A feeling Rafe couldn't define pushed against his chest,

demanding space, hurting in its intensity. A violent shudder went through him, and he pressed his face into Genny's hair.

She smelled of life, Genny did.

Rage burned in him that she had been forced into danger. The fury quietened as she began to stroke his shoulder, his neck, his jaw.

He closed his eyes. Her touch spread warmth, thawing places in him that nothing else could penetrate. He was fully aroused, filled with desire.

With danger all around, he knew it was normal to seek an affirmation of life. But making love with Genny brought its own kind of danger. Her warmth might dissolve the most solid of glaciers. But then what?

He didn't know.

Another shudder went through him. All he knew was that his need for her was greater than his need for survival....

Dear Reader,

Welcome to Silhouette Special Edition . . . welcome to romance. We've got six wonderful books for you this month—a true bouquet of spring flowers!

Just Hold On Tight! by Andrea Edwards is our THAT SPECIAL WOMAN! selection for this month. This warm, poignant story features a heroine who longs for love—and the wonderful man who convinces her to take what she needs!

And that's not all! *Dangerous Alliance,* the next installment in Lindsay McKenna's thrilling new series MEN OF COURAGE, is available this month, as well as Christine Rimmer's *Man of the Mountain,* the first story in the family-oriented series THE JONES GANG. Sherryl Woods keeps us up-to-date on the Halloran clan in *A Vow To Love,* and *Wild Is the Wind,* by Laurie Paige, brings us back to "Wild River" territory for an exciting new tale of love.

May also welcomes Noreen Brownlie to Silhouette Special Edition with her book, *That Outlaw Attitude.*

I hope that you enjoy this book and all of the stories to come.

Happy Spring!

Sincerely,

Tara Gavin
Senior Editor

Please address questions and book requests to:
Reader Service
U.S.: P.O. Box 1325, Buffalo, NY 14269
Canadian: P.O. Box 1050, Niagara Falls, Ont. L2E 7G7

LAURIE PAIGE

WILD IS THE WIND

Published by Silhouette Books
America's Publisher of Contemporary Romance

To Tanner, who's off to see the world

ISBN 0-373-09887-1

WILD IS THE WIND

This edition published by arrangement with Harlequin Enterprises B. V.

Printed in U.S.A.

Books by Laurie Paige

Silhouette Special Edition

Lover's Choice #170
Man Without a Past #755
†*Home for a Wild Heart* #828
†*A Place for Eagles* #839
†*The Way of a Man* #849
†*Wild Is the Wind* #887

†Wild River series

Silhouette Desire

Gypsy Enchantment #123
Journey to Desire #195
Misty Splendor #304
Golden Promise #404

Silhouette Romance

South of the Sun #296
A Tangle of Rainbows #333
A Season for Butterflies #364
Nothing Lost #382
The Sea at Dawn #398
A Season for Homecoming #727
Home Fires Burning Bright #733
Man from the North Country #772
**Cara's Beloved* #917
**Sally's Beau* #923
**Victoria's Conquest* #933
Caleb's Son #994

*All-American Sweethearts

LAURIE PAIGE

Sometimes an idea catches the imagination and won't let go. That happened eight years ago when I read about a pair of eagles in a nature magazine. I knew right then that I'd write the "eagle" story someday. Each time I'd come up with a hero and heroine, I'd wonder, "Is this the eagle story?" It wasn't until I visited the Rogue River that it all came together—the eagle theme, the story ideas (like a lightning storm my husband and I witnessed there, several stories hit me at once) and the characters. Every part of the river was grist for a story—ranches, logging operations, pear orchards, resorts, towns and fishing villages. It was going to take more than one book to tell them all. And so the Wild River series began....

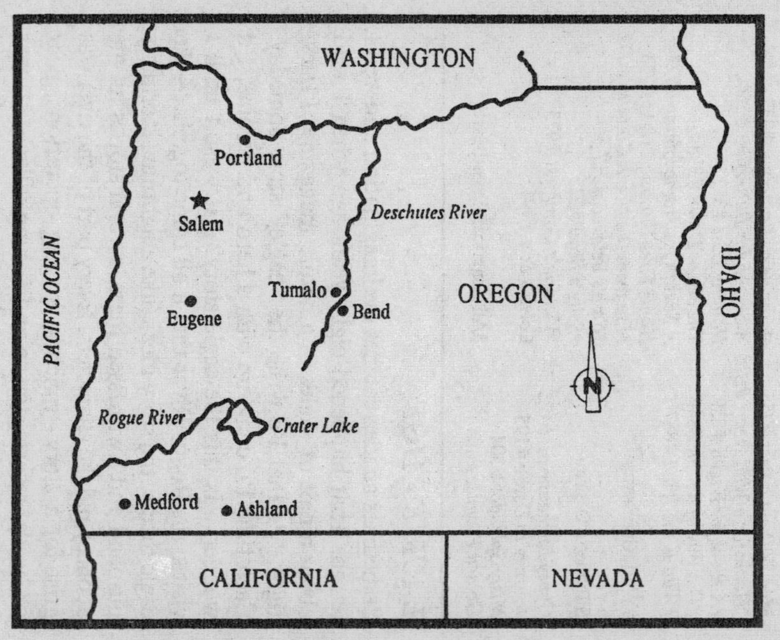
WASHINGTON
Portland
Salem
Deschutes River
PACIFIC OCEAN
Tumalo
Bend
Eugene
OREGON
IDAHO
N
Rogue River
Crater Lake
Medford
Ashland
CALIFORNIA
NEVADA

Chapter One

Rafe Barrett stamped the snow off his boots. He went through the double set of insulated doors, then stepped into the warmth of the wood-and-stone lodge at the Rogue Mountain Resort, once known as the Moose Creek Inn.

He'd been running the resort—jointly owned with his sister Rachel McPherson, who had married a rancher and lived about fifty miles up the Rogue River from there—for three years now.

Glancing around the two-story foyer, which was flanked by shops of all kinds, he spotted the maintenance supervisor flirting with one of the salesgirls in the expensive boutique next to the souvenir shop.

"Bill, could I see you for a moment?" Rafe called.

The supervisor was divorced, in his forties, with a lean, craggy face and a good build. He liked to tease the female help.

"Sure," Bill said easily. With a smile and a nod, he left the salesclerk and crossed the foyer to his boss. "What's up?"

"The path to the town houses has a foot of snow on it."

Bill frowned. "Hmm, that was supposed to have been blown off around midnight and again at six this morning. I'll check on it."

"Pete's usually reliable," Rafe commented.

"Yeah, but he's laid up with the flu. A new guy was assigned to do it. I'll see what his problem is."

"Do that. I don't want to start the season with the condo guests angry. We have a full house there."

It was the Friday after Thanksgiving, and they'd had their first deep snow of the season that week.

"The lodge is booked for the weekend, too," Bill told him. "Only the A-frames have a couple of vacancies."

Rafe nodded. "Maybe this will be a decent season for a change." After a three-year drought with little snow and few skiers, they needed all the help they could get.

"Right. The early snow is getting us off to a good start. I have a feeling it's a sign of the future. We'll be skiing right into June this year." Bill gave him a half salute and headed toward the offices located at the back of the lodge.

Rafe watched him go, wryly hoping the prediction was reliable, then glanced back at the boutique. The salesclerk smiled at him in that half-shy, half-coy manner he'd become accustomed to since he'd taken over the running of the resort. He smiled back, friendly but remote...an employer's smile, nothing more.

Disappointment dampened her expression. She turned to the counter and straightened a rack of brightly colored earrings.

Briefly, he wondered where Valerie, his assistant manager, found the people she hired during the busy periods.

Both men and women seemed cloned from the same type—young, good-looking, athletic. At thirty-five, he felt ancient by comparison.

He started for his office, then stopped dead still as a low, tantalizing murmur of laughter caressed his ears. He stood unmoving, every nerve in his body taut, but the husky, melodious sound didn't come again.

Inside him, his heart set up a harsh, heavy beat while his throat closed as memory flooded over him.

Genny's laughter...like the softly drawn notes of a flute on the early morning desert air... clear and haunting....

"Are you all right? Mr. Barrett? You okay?"

He glanced around. The young clerk stood at the door of the boutique, staring at him curiously.

"Yes," he snapped.

She visibly recoiled at his sharp reply.

"Sorry," he muttered. "I, uh, just thought of something," he added vaguely to explain his sudden trance. He hurried to his office. Work, with all its annoying details, would set thoughts of Genny aside.

But in his office he ignored the telephone messages and the letters that needed his attention.

Genny.

He'd hardly thought of her in years...hadn't allowed himself to think of her. The memories always brought pain. They whispered to him of death.

And betrayal. *He* should have died, not Tom. Tom... his best friend. Tom...who had been in love with Genny.

Rafe hadn't been able to face her after the funeral, although he'd held her while she'd cried during the ordeal. A shuddering sigh ripped through him. It had been better to leave, to sever all connections between them right then.

The ringing of the telephone stopped his morbid thoughts. He grabbed the receiver up like a lifeline that would pull him safely back to sanity and his ordered life.

At noon, after consulting with Val on the weekend bookings, Rafe went to lunch, satisfied that all was well with the world he'd carved out for himself. He'd taken a money-losing resort and put it on its feet and on the map, so to speak.

The dining room was nearly empty. Tonight it would be full to overflowing when the skiers started arriving, eager to test their skills against the snow-covered slopes in the morning.

He went to his favorite spot, a table for two tucked away in the back corner next to the last section of double-pane picture windows. The view was magnificent, a place where the spirit could soar and the heart could heal....

He frowned at the odd thought. There was nothing wrong with his spirit or his heart. Not a thing. He focused on the view again and ignored such nonsense.

Rogue Mountain was one of the tallest peaks in the area. From there, he could see fifty miles out and a thousand feet down into the Rogue Valley of southern Oregon. The river gleamed like a silver necklace against the throat of the curving valley.

He glanced up when the waitress came over. A movement at the entrance caught his eye. He glimpsed the back of a woman as she left the restaurant. His heart stopped, then beat heavily.

That dark fall of hair, thick and wavy, was like Genny's. The set of the woman's shoulders was familiar. They were somewhat broad for a female, but feminine because that was the way Genny was—feminine and so very beautiful.

The earlier pain returned, grabbed him by the heart and yanked. He gritted his teeth and cursed silently.

Forget the past. What was done, was done. Nothing he could do would change what had happened. Nothing.

"We have a grilled mahimahi salad special today, Rafe," the waitress told him. "It's really good."

"I'll take it." His voice came out husky with strain. He cleared it impatiently and managed a pleasant grin. He hoped.

After the waitress brought his coffee, he tried to concentrate on the new projects he had going. He'd added snow-making equipment to one long intermediate slope, including the side runs off it. That should keep the resort open even when the weather didn't cooperate.

His mind stubbornly returned to its own musing, and he wondered why the woman with the dark hair had left the restaurant in such a hurry. Presumably she'd come upstairs intending to eat, then had remembered something important.... Or maybe she'd just gotten lost...or had been looking for someone.

He sipped the hot coffee and recalled his first meeting with Genny....

"Hello," she'd said, holding out her hand.

Her smile had been open, generous. A haze of moisture had clung to her upper lip in the intense heat of the desert. She'd worn a long-sleeved white blouse, buttoned almost to the neck. Her split skirt had reached to the ankles of her riding boots.

They were guests of a sheikh, and Rafe had admired the demure way in which she'd dressed in deference to the modesty of the sheikh's wife and several daughters.

"You must be Genevieve," Rafe had said.

"Yes, but please call me Genny." Her eyes were the clear, golden green of new grass.

He'd taken an instant liking to her. There had been something so open, so generous in her smile....

"Ah, you've found him," Tom had said, coming into the enclosed garden. He'd dropped a possessive arm around her shoulders. "Rafe Barrett, Genevieve McBride," he'd introduced them.

Tom had talked incessantly about his old high school flame upon his return from Paris. The reality was more than Rafe had expected. With an effort, he'd looked away from her.

The sheikh's home was on a lake created by a dam, part of a desert reclamation project. The area was an oasis of palm and acacia trees, of secret walled gardens with sparkling fountains that delighted the senses. Beyond the lake, the rugged landscape stretched to the horizon in limitless sand and pale scrub.

Rafe had wondered if she would like the desert and its vast expanse of sand and scrub. He hadn't asked. Instead he'd smiled politely, shaken her hand and released it. He'd answered her questions about the success of the reclamation project, aware that he'd made a big mistake in allowing her there.

He had been in charge of a diplomatic mission to coordinate summit talks between two warring desert factions. Tom had asked him to request Genny as the translator. It had seemed a sensible thing to do. Her credentials were impeccable, and she'd been available.

He'd miscalculated. Her file hadn't mentioned the way her mouth curled up at the corners when she smiled or the way she tilted her head when she looked at him. Nor had he been prepared for his relief when Tom confided he wasn't making any headway in recapturing the interest of his long-ago steady.

Meeting her had been like stepping into the sun after a long winter of unbearable cold. Genny and the desert sun—they'd forever be linked in his mind. Genny and her incredible warmth.

Rafe clenched the handle of the cup until his knuckles went white. The need for that warmth had never left him.

"Here you are."

Rafe looked at the plate of grilled fish and the colorful assortment of salad greens and vegetables the waitress put in front of him. "Thanks," he said.

Food wasn't what he needed. He wasn't sure what he did want, only that a need stirred in him whenever he thought of Genny.

Like today, he admitted. Laughter, a swath of dark hair—it took very little to bring her to mind. It had been almost three years since she'd driven him to the plane that had taken him out of her life. Neither had spoken much. It had been a sad day, the day after the funeral back in the hometown where she and Tom had grown up next door to each other.

Rafe wondered if she'd ever found out it had been his fault that Tom had died.

Genny hurried along the winding path that meandered through the poplars and silver birches. A few golden leaves still clung to their branches. It had been a funny fall—warm right up until the snowstorm had come roaring in earlier that week. The trees had barely slipped into their autumn finery when the blizzard had hit.

She paused at the door of an A-frame chalet and looked behind her. The trail was empty. She quickly went in, slammed the door against the cold and dropped into the oversize easy chair.

Her heart pounded, and she panted as if she'd run from some grave, invisible danger.

Rafe Barrett. There was danger enough.

Would he want to see her? She had been trying to get up the courage to approach his office when she'd seen him leave it. She'd followed him upstairs to the restaurant. But then she'd lost her nerve. He'd looked so... formidable. The way he'd been the last time they were together. She'd sent him Christmas cards for the past three years, but he'd never responded.

She pressed her hands to her eyes to stop the emotion that welled up in spite of her attempts to hold it at bay. It had been so long since she'd seen him. She hadn't realized he would still affect her this way.

Gradually she calmed down, then rose to her feet. She had to face him sometime. But not this minute. After washing her face and combing her hair, she put on a light dusting of makeup.

Camouflage, she thought wryly as she brushed subtle color around her eyes. Putting on a "new" face was a woman's way of hiding her emotions from the world.

Men hid behind anger and a brusque manner. Or maybe they refused to think about things that hurt. Pretend it doesn't exist and maybe it'll go away. Like the attraction she and Rafe had felt from the first instant of meeting.

After Tom's death, by a bomb planted in the car, Rafe had become as cold and distant as a glacier, even when he'd held her while she'd cried. He'd never called or written after he'd left.

She had returned to Paris. This was her first trip to the States since Tom's funeral. Tom, her childhood friend. The boy next door. He'd wanted to be an ambassador, like her uncle, like Rafe's father. He'd had such ambition, so many grand plans.

But even the grandest schemes could fail, she thought, a tremor of apprehension going through her.

Her reasons for being at a ski resort in southern Oregon instead of at her desk in Paris were twofold. One, a dealer in illegal arms—the man responsible for the bomb in the embassy car—had escaped from prison and put out a contract on the people instrumental in sending him there. She was one of those people. The State Department had decided she needed a safe house.

Her second reason concerned Rafe. He, too, had been involved in solving the case. He had refused protection.

Presumably, with her safety at stake, Rafe would accept the inevitable. Or so Rafe's father, along with a gentle nudge from her uncle, had persuaded her. Rafe's sense of responsibility would force him to endure her presence and aid in her protection, even if he did tend to disregard his own safety.

There was a third reason, she admitted. It was personal.

She put the little case of eye shadow aside and turned from the mirror. Seeing Rafe again had stirred up all the emotions of the past. Well, what had she expected?

After clipping the small tote pack she used for a purse around her waist, she slipped into a parka and went for a hike along a snow-covered trail. An hour later she emerged from the woods onto a dais of granite.

In one direction, she could see the lodge sitting on the side of the mountain, its windows sparkling in the sun.

In the other direction, the river, known for the pear orchards that lined its banks in this section, swept toward the sea. Beyond the far bend, the valley narrowed into steep gorges and sharp ravines, and the river became swift and dangerous . . . a wild river that lived up to its name—the Rogue.

A cloud scurried over the sun, and the air chilled. She zipped the parka to her neck and stuck her hands deep into her pockets. A strange feeling pervaded her, a premonition of danger and other things she couldn't define.

A point had been reached in her life. Events had been set in motion. From here, her destiny would change, as it had after that desert visit, but for better or for worse, she didn't know.

She glanced over the majestic sweep of mountains with their pure white covering of snow. It was beautiful—peaceful and serene, not at all how she felt.

Rafe glanced out the window. The sky had darkened. Clouds totally obscured the sun. Although the time was only a little after four, it seemed as if twilight was at hand. While he watched, a scattering of tiny snowflakes began to sift down.

He'd hoped they'd have sunny weather for the first ski weekend of the season, but it looked like they were in for a storm. He stood, stretched and yawned, then locked his desk and headed out.

"You gone for the day?" Val asked, removing her glasses and laying them on the cluttered desk when he stuck his head around the edge of her door.

"Yeah. See you tomorrow."

"Right. Have a nice evening. Oh, if you have time, check out the new band in the Moosehead tonight."

He waved a hand to tell her he'd heard her, but didn't make a commitment. He didn't feel like company tonight. The bar was popular with the younger crowd...and fifty-year-old men trying to make it with the twenty-two-year-old chicks.

A few more years and that's probably where he'd be—pretending to a youth he didn't have just to impress some female. But not tonight. Tonight he'd sleep alone and try not to dream of Genny.

Pulling on a dark blue down-filled vest, he was in the process of zipping it—the damned thing just wouldn't connect right—as he headed out into the crystal-cold air. His breath alternately appeared and disappeared in front of his face.

He still hadn't gotten the zipper to work when he reached the point where the path divided. He heard running footsteps and looked up just in time to see a brightly clad form hurdling at him, head down, arms pumping. The runner crashed into him before he could react.

The force of the impact rocked him back on his heels, but he was able to handle the jolt. He caught the woman's shoulders and steadied them both. She looked up, obviously startled.

He stared into eyes the color of new grass—a soft, light green with a golden tinge. "My God," he muttered.

"Rafe," Genny said. She felt as stunned as he looked. Her heart seemed to fill her throat and she could say no more. This wasn't how she had envisioned the meeting.

She wanted to be calm, in control. She wanted to walk up to him with a smile and a planned greeting, not careen into him like an adolescent out of control.

"Hello," she finally said. She smiled and felt her lips tremble. She wanted to reach up and kiss him.

"Genny," he said in a low tone like the warning growl of a cornered wolf. His grip tightened painfully on her.

She couldn't stop looking at him. He wore jeans with a dark, royal-blue turtleneck and a Norwegian cable-knit sweater, white with a blue and green pattern woven in. Over the sweater, he wore a vest that matched the turtleneck.

His hair was light brown with golden highlights, its tones warm like toast with butter. His eyes were brown at the outer edges, then green flecked with gold toward the center. When he'd seen who she was, they'd narrowed in loathing.

She swallowed as her nerves stretched to the breaking point. He saw the movement and stared at her throat for a second before coming back to her eyes.

"What are you doing here?" he demanded.

"I'm on...v-vacation," she stammered, all her rehearsed lines going right out of her head.

"Vacation," he repeated. A scowl settled between his eyes.

"Uh, yes. My...uncle thought I'd been working too hard and needed a rest." Actually, Uncle Sam was paying for this visit. She was on a working vacation, one might say.

He looked as if he thought this was an out-and-out lie, but he didn't dispute it.

"You're hurting me," she said.

He released the death grip on her shoulders, but remained where he was, blocking her path to the chalet. He gave a low curse, then took her wrist. "Come on," he ordered.

"Where are we going?" she asked several minutes later as he guided her along the path at a rapid clip.

"My place."

The snow crunched under their feet as they walked. Around them, downy flakes swirled in the breeze like tiny feathers blown by a playful giant. The storm enclosed them in its icy embrace. She looked around. No one in sight. She and Rafe were alone.

Her nerves tightened in alarm.

A sniper could easily hide in the woods, shoot them as they passed, then take off without anyone seeing him.

Genny shook off the thought. According to the latest information, the hired gun wasn't even in the country yet. She observed the area, noting every feature of the terrain and each building they passed.

The town houses were arranged in groups of four to a building, each building set at an angle to the others on the hillside. There were ten buildings, each surrounded by yew bushes and pine trees.

The snow chattered against the pine needles with a sound like the busy clicking of a hundred knitting needles.

A chill crept down her neck. This meeting with Rafe was going to be harder than she'd thought. So much time had passed.

The path climbed rather steeply now. She struggled to keep up with Rafe's long stride. They reached the last building, the highest one. Naturally, the eagle would have an aerie.

She glanced at his hair. A golden eagle. The image suited, she realized. She wondered if he was ever lonely.

They went up a broad flight of steps, the first five of metal grid to let the snow fall through, the last five of wood. He opened a storm door and let her precede him onto the sun porch, which was enclosed in glass; then he unlocked the door into the town house and again waited for her to enter.

The interior was a surprise. She stopped in the middle of the floor, which was tiled with green slate squares.

The kitchen was papered in a leafy print of pale teal green with white cabinets and sandstone-colored countertops. A random number of the sandstone backsplash tiles were printed with examples of common herbs.

Padded wooden benches were built under the bank of windows at either side of the door they'd entered. The benches could be used for storage and seating. Cushions of green, beige and bright peach were piled into the corners at each end of the benches. An oak table was to her left, a stairwell to her right side.

"Rafe, this is charming," she exclaimed. "It's perfect for entertaining. And for a family."

A picture of Rafe as a father came to her, bending over the table, helping a son or daughter with homework.

She'd seen him hold a child. His touch could be so gentle. She knew. He'd once kissed her with such tenderness, his passion held in check as they caressed and explored, that she'd almost wept with joy—

"This way," he said, breaking into the memory.

She blinked the image from her mind and followed him into the adjoining room, a flagstone walkway, which enclosed an atrium on four sides. She realized the house had been built around the glassed-in garden. A tall, slender tree and several plants reached toward the skylights two stories above them.

A den opened off the natural stone walkway to the right. The living room was opposite the kitchen, and she got a glimpse of a bedroom on the left side. She assumed the doors off the balcony above her opened on to guest bedrooms and baths.

He used the den as an alternate office, she saw. The desk was littered with papers, brochures and magazines. Two small sofas flanked a natural stone fireplace. A throw pillow and an afghan suggested afternoon naps before the fire.

She drew a shaky breath and looked away.

He indicated she should be seated. When she was, he demanded, "Now tell me what the hell you're doing here."

She longed to tell him the truth, the real one and the personal one. She wanted to ask why he'd never come to her.

Spreading her hands in an open, candid gesture, she opted for part of the truth. "I told you. I needed a vacation. I haven't taken any time off since..." Her voice trailed off.

"Since Tom died," Rafe finished for her, his tone grim.

"Yes," she said. "I could use some coffee. It was colder than I realized when I hiked out to the point. I didn't eat lunch," she remembered, then wished she hadn't spoken.

"It *was* you," he said, his eyes narrowing on her again. "At the restaurant earlier. You left. Because you saw me?"

She nodded. "I knew we'd see each other eventually, but I found I wasn't... ready."

He uttered a low sound in the back of his throat, a growl of disbelief or contempt, she wasn't sure which. Without speaking, he walked out of the room.

She heard him in the kitchen—the splash of water and the clink of glass as he put the coffee on to brew. When he didn't immediately return, she rose and went into the atrium hall.

Rafe was making sandwiches, quickly and efficiently cutting thin slices off a baked ham. She attributed the emptiness she felt to lack of food, but that wasn't all it was.

Watching him, she felt the aching hunger grow inside her, not for food, but for *him*. During the six weeks she'd spent in the desert, she'd learned to listen for him—for the deep, pleasant rumble of his voice in the clear, cool morning air, for his laughter, quick and joyous, for his knock on her door just as the sun rose, calling her to ride with him over the dunes....

She turned from watching him and looked into the atrium, studying the various plants as if she'd never seen them before.

Until she'd met Rafe, she hadn't realized there were so many ways of loving. She'd loved Tom. They'd grown up together, had gone steady during high school, then had drifted apart when he'd left for college, only to meet again in Paris where she had taken a position on the embassy staff.

When Tom had learned she was available for temporary work wherever she was needed, he'd been delighted. He had gotten her assigned to the desert project. He'd also wanted to resume their youthful romance, but she had refused. While she liked and admired him, there was something missing in her feelings for him.

From Rafe she'd learned what passion truly meant. They hadn't made love, but their kisses had been so intense she'd felt scorched by the heat of their longing.

Rafe had made her feel beautiful, tempestuous. He had made her soar with his glance, had made her dizzy with his touch, had filled her with yearning. And an enduring tenderness.

Footsteps caused her to look up. Rafe carried a full plate in each hand. He gave one to her, then went into the den and set his down on the coffee table between the two sofas. He returned to the kitchen for the coffee.

Genny went into the den and settled on one of the buttery smooth sofas. The leather was light beige, the rug an Indian design on a sandstone background, the floors of golden oak. Pottery vases on the bookcases had vivid splashes of turquoise.

Rafe brought in the coffee, placed the tray on the table and sat opposite her on the matching sofa. Her glance went to the hearth. A crackling fire would be all they needed to set the scene for a romantic interlude.

"I turned the thermostat up. The place should be warm in a minute," he said.

She realized she still had on her parka. He'd taken his vest off in the kitchen. The Nordic sweater looked ruggedly handsome on him. He could have been a Viking, she decided.

She shrugged out of her coat and laid it aside, then picked up the sandwich and took a bite. He'd added carrot sticks and chips to the plate.

"This is very good," she said after a couple of minutes with only the whisper of the snowflakes hitting the window to break the strained silence.

During the six weeks in the desert, they'd talked constantly, the ideas spilling from them like water from a spring. They'd had so much to say, they'd often spoken at the same time, their words rushing over each other in a duet of exploration and sharing of experiences. Now her mind had gone blank.

He finished his meal first.

Her stomach tightened when he leaned back, draped an arm over the sofa back and watched her with a suspicious gaze. She quickly polished off the rest of the sandwich and carrots and chips.

"Now are you ready to talk?" he asked, an ominous quiet in his tone.

Genny nodded. She'd stick to her story. It was the truth, but not all of it.

"It's simple, really," she began. "I picked up a bug when I was sent to Egypt recently—"

"You were on a job?"

"Yes, some translations and summaries of several documents my uncle wanted me to do."

She spoke Arabic, Hebrew and several African dialects, as well as French and Italian. Her parents had realized early that languages came easily for her. A gift. They'd encouraged her to develop it. Her uncle had asked her to join the diplomatic corps when she finished her master's degree in linguistics.

"Are you still located in Paris?" Rafe wanted to know.

"Sort of."

He gave her an inquiring look.

"I'm on leave. To recover completely, rest up and, perhaps, to decide what I want to do with the rest of my life. I recently turned thirty."

"I remember."

She looked at him and saw that he did. All the memories that had haunted her had also haunted him. It was strange to be so connected to one person and yet so far apart.

His doing, she reminded herself. She'd known they needed some time apart, a time to grieve and a time to heal, but Rafe had never called or written, not once. Had she been wrong about the depth of their feelings there in the magic of the desert?

A frisson skipped along her nerves. There was tension in the room. And awareness. *That* was why she was here.

When her uncle and Rafe's father had urged her to come to the resort after she was dismissed from the hospital, she'd first been wary and uncertain because Rafe had never contacted her, but the leap of her heart had told her this was something she needed to resolve—the feelings she had for this man.

"This seemed like the ideal place to relax and think about the future," she elaborated when the silence grew too long for comfort.

"Liar," he said.

Chapter Two

"Explain that," Genny requested, outwardly composed.

"I know why you're here." He clenched his fists, his face grim as death.

She swallowed against the knot that filled her throat, wondering if he really had any idea. "I've told you why. It's the truth," she declared.

He picked up his cup of coffee and stared into its steamy depths for a minute, as if reading their future. "You're here because you need a safe house."

Genny couldn't prevent the guilty jerk of her hands on her cup. She mopped up the few spilled drops with a napkin.

"Well..." she began.

His face hardened. "Don't bother denying it. You're a terrible liar."

"I know," she agreed softly, sadly.

When Tom had accused her of being attracted to Rafe, she hadn't been able to deny it. Even though she'd given Tom no reason to think there was more than friendship between them, he'd seemed to think she belonged to him.

In Paris, that most romantic of cities, he'd tried to rush her into a commitment. She'd refused. Later, during the desert trip, she'd told him she would never love him as more than a friend. He'd been furious with her. Rafe was furious with her now.

"Why do you need a place to hide?" Rafe demanded.

She pondered making something up, but found she couldn't lie to him. "I translated some letters, remembered a similarity to other documents I'd read—it was the way the writer used words, the syntax and things like that—and discovered an embassy clerk had a deal going with some international crooks. They were caught, but a contract was put out—"

Rafe set the cup down so hard she wondered that it didn't break. He stood and strode about the room, cursing eloquently.

At last he stopped in front of her. "Does your uncle know where you were sent?"

She nodded. "He suggested it."

Rafe muttered something under his breath. "Why would anyone in his right mind think you'd be safe here?"

"Why wouldn't I be?" she countered, surprised by the question.

He glared at her as if she were lamebrain. "Because any idiot could find out that you and I had once worked together, or that your uncle and my father, both ambassadors to troubled areas, are friends."

"But you and I haven't seen each other in almost three years," she reminded him. A note of censure crept into her voice.

Why? she wanted to ask. Why didn't you ever come to me?

"We haven't even been on the same continent," she added. His choice, not hers. A sense of desolation washed over her. She couldn't figure out what she'd done to turn him away.

"Who's watching you?"

"There's an agent—"

"One?" He cursed again, consigning his father, her uncle, the State Department and the government in general to Hades. "How the hell can one agent protect a person?"

"He knows the contract man," she explained.

Rafe swore again.

"I never realized you had such an extensive vocabulary," she remarked, smiling in spite of the seriousness of the situation.

He paused in his tirade and glared at her. Gradually his expression changed. She realized he was staring at her mouth.

Heat spread throughout her. She wondered what he was thinking...if he was remembering how they had kissed there in the desert, locked together in a storm of desire...

"Do you think being stalked by a killer is a joke?" The harshness of his tone interrupted her daydream.

"No," she replied steadily. "But I think there may be worse things than death."

The silence built between them.

"Like what?" he finally asked.

"Loneliness," she suggested. "Or needing someone and being turned away without a backward glance."

His gaze narrowed to slits. He looked wary and dangerous. Hard. Unreachable. "Are you here to finish what we started in the desert that day...the day that Tom died?"

The cruelty of the question shook her composure. "No," she said, going over her feelings and motives while she spoke, "but I wanted to see you again."

He sucked in a quick breath. "You're honest, I'll give you that." His expression changed abruptly. "Where are you staying? In the lodge?"

"No, in a chalet."

"Those are too isolated. The lodge would be better." He paced the room again. "Is the guard staying with you?"

"No."

Rafe shook his head. "Then how the hell is he supposed to keep someone from slipping in and quietly cutting your throat?"

At her look of surprise, he groaned. She obviously hadn't thought the consequences through. Neither had her guard, it seemed. Some protection she was getting. He had a thing or two to say to the head of this operation when he saw the man.

"The lodge is full for the weekend. We can move you over first thing Monday morning. The question is, where can we put you in the meantime?"

She looked at him silently, her gaze expectantly on him. Just like a woman, he thought. They caused the problem, then sat back and waited for a man to figure out the solution.

She could stay with him.

He blocked the thought, but it was too late. It stuck in his mind. And it was the sensible thing to do at this late date.

"They should have asked me," he muttered.

"My uncle said they did." She met his gaze without a trace of emotion on her face.

A feeling like a red-hot knife going into his vitals attacked him. His father had called him about using the resort as a safe house for a few days. Rafe had okayed the plan, but only on the proviso that their agent take care of everything and leave him out of it. When he'd left the diplomatic corps, he'd made it clear he wanted nothing to do with international intrigue ever again.

He glanced at his unexpected guest. No one had said it was Genny who needed a bolt hole. Hell, there were a thousand places they could have sent her. Why here?

He clamped down on the emotions that rioted through him at the thought of her in danger. Now was not the time for personal feelings. A man had to stay emotionally uninvolved to make wise decisions. He'd failed in that once. Never again.

"I told them I didn't want anything to do with the operation. A lot of good it did me." He paused. "No one said it was you."

"If you'd known it was me, would you have still said yes?"

She sounded . . . wistful. He ignored the rush of feeling that went through him and reminded himself of the blunt realities of the past as well as the present.

Because of her, he'd betrayed his best friend, knowing Tom was in love with Genny and trying to win her. Because he'd wanted to be with her, he'd let Tom take the car and meet the arriving VIP. Because of his lust for this woman, a good man had died in his place. He'd never forgive himself for that.

"No," he said. "I don't want you here."

* * *

Genny finished packing and closed the suitcase. Rafe and a bellhop from the lodge stood by, ready to take her things to Rafe's home when she was ready.

She looked around, checking the bathroom and bureaus once more. "That's it, I think."

The bellhop picked up the large suitcase. Rafe carried her suitbag and overnight case. She clipped her tote around her waist and slipped into her coat and thick gloves. It was dark out now and deadly cold, the temperature around zero.

The wind took her breath when she stepped outside behind the two men. It whipped the warmth away from her body. Windchill, she thought. It made her shiver. Like Rafe's eyes.

I don't want you here.

Nothing could be plainer. She sighed and wrapped her arms across her chest as she trudged uphill against the wind. In spite of Rafe's anger, the plan was working.

So far, it had been easy. Rafe might have refused protection for himself, but Mr. Barrett had known his son well.

"He'll take you under his wing," the ambassador had predicted. "He'll work with our man for your sake. I'm asking you to do this for mine. I worry about my son. He's a lonely man." He'd paused. "Rafe and his sister are close. Rachel says he was once in love with someone... someone he met three years ago."

Genny hadn't been able to forget the implications of Mr. Barrett's statement. So here she was, a refugee from all she'd previously known, a woman with undefined feelings for a man who obviously equated her with a painful time in his own life and wanted only to forget her.

The three of them tramped up the ten steps to the front porch, stomping the snow off their boots as they went. Rafe led the way inside. "Put the bag down there," he ordered the younger man.

He gave the guy a tip, saw him out, then slammed and locked the door with the dead bolt. He handed her the overnight case and picked up the larger bag.

Again she followed while he led the way upstairs, around the balcony lining the atrium and into a bedroom of peach and pale green tones.

"There's a bath through there and a sitting room on the other side of that," Rafe pointed out. He set her luggage down on a mahogany captain's chest with bronze hardware. Bronze table lamps stood sentinel on each side of the bed. The bedspread, drapes and easy chair were done in a peach and green floral print with the soft, misty look of a watercolor.

"I feel as if this room were made for me," she murmured. She felt strange inside...as if she'd finally come home.

Her hands trembled when she set the overnight case down and slipped out of her parka. She removed the tote from around her waist and laid it on the small reading table beside the chair.

Letting her fingers trail over the table, the chair, the silky feel of the sheer curtains under the drapes, she wandered around the spacious room, bemused by feelings she couldn't explain.

"This house could have been designed for me."

Rafe gave her a cool glance. "It was built ten years ago. I had it remodeled when I moved in. A professional designer did the interior with no help from me."

"Yes. It shows an elegant touch. Designers aren't afraid to use color. Your home is beautiful," she said sincerely.

The moment intensified as he stared into her eyes. He seemed to be searching her soul for answers to questions only he knew. She held herself still and open to him.

He broke the connection and headed for the door. "I'll heat some soup for supper. Come down when you're through up here."

She was disappointed when he left. Sitting in the comfortable chair, she pondered the situation between them. There were feelings between them, undercurrents of emotion that had existed from the first moment. But what emotions?

Attraction? Yes.

Desire? Yes.

Love? A harder question.

That was what she was really here to find out, she admitted. Anything else was an excuse. She could have gone anywhere and been just as safe. Rafe could have been watched without his knowing.

Gabriel Deveraux, the agent assigned to the case, was one of the best. He knew how the American expatriate—a man who sold his deadly services to the highest bidder—operated.

Sighing at the complexity of life, she opened her cases and set about unpacking for the second time that day. When she went downstairs, the smell of homemade soup made her realize that the sandwich she'd eaten—she glanced at the kitchen clock—more than two hours ago was gone and she was hungry again.

"Mountain air must be wonderful for the appetite," she commented to her host, who stood with his hands in his pockets, gazing out the broad bank of windows toward the valley.

He flicked her a glance when she stopped beside him. "Yeah."

"The view is outstanding from here. In the spring, with the fruit trees in bloom, the valley must look like a wonderland."

He gave a grunt, which she took for agreement.

"I imagine it's lovely in summer, too. And in the fall with all the trees changing color—the birches and poplars and pears." She heard herself rattling on inanely, and realized how nervous she was now that she was in the lion's den, so to speak.

"Yes, lovely," he said, his voice low and deep.

Her eyes were drawn to his. Her breathing grew labored as he looked at her with the heated passion she'd seen three years ago in his eyes. Then it was gone.

He went to the stove and served up the soup. From the oven, he removed a loaf of French bread and put it in a basket. Genny went to help him bring the meal to the table.

When they were seated, she picked up her spoon and tasted the soup. "This is delicious," she exclaimed.

"Don't look so surprised. Women aren't the only members of the human race who can cook." His smile was sardonic.

Her own was radiant. "Did that sound sexist? Sorry. I just never pictured you as the domestic type. Did you really make it yourself?"

"All by my lonesome," he avowed. "At night, I usually prefer to eat in rather than go to the lodge or the Moosehead."

The Moosehead Bar and Grill was a restaurant and bar farther down the mountain, tucked into a rise where Moose Creek meandered by on its way to the Rogue. There was dancing on the weekends, she'd read in one of the brochures when she'd arrived.

She looked at the silent, formidable man across the table from her. Would she ever dance in his arms again? Suddenly she was swept back in time to a night three weeks after she'd met Rafe.

Their host, a diplomat like her uncle, had held a party. There had been dancing girls as part of the entertainment. She'd watched Rafe looking at them, a smile of appreciation on his mobile lips, and had been jealous.

Jealous!

It had been such a shock. Shaken, she'd excused herself early and gone to her room. Unable to sleep, she'd slipped on satin scuffs and a silk chiffon robe over her nightgown and walked around the high wall of the garden.

Rafe had joined her there, startling her but not really surprising her when he'd stepped out from the shadows. Silently they'd danced to the music coming from the ongoing party, their eyes locked together as their bodies moved closer and closer—

"Stop it," a voice interrupted her musing.

Her hand jerked, spilling the spoon of hot soup back into the bowl. "Stop what?" she asked breathlessly.

"Remembering."

Heat flooded her, not all of it from embarrassment that he'd read her so easily.

She could stop the images, but she couldn't stop the memory of his arms holding her, drawing her close so that her breasts pressed against him with only thin layers of silk and cotton between. The night had been pleasantly warm as the breeze from the desert blew across them.

Looking out the window at the snow that still tumbled down from a cloudy sky, she thought of the desert moon. How bright it had been. How big, floating like a circle of silver above them.

"A time out of time," she murmured, feeling the elements surround and isolate them in the snowstorm the way they had that night in the desert.

"One that'll never come again," he said with a brusqueness she'd never heard from him.

"I know." The sadness crept into her soul like the cold crept into the cabin.

"I'll call headquarters tomorrow. You'll stay here only until arrangements for another place can be made. Anywhere in the States should be safe."

She nodded and continued eating, keeping her face blank, her emotions shaky but controlled. His desire to get rid of her was harder to take than she'd thought it would be.

Rising abruptly, he took his bowl to the sink, rinsed it and stored it in the dishwasher. "There's a fire in the den when you're finished." He walked out.

Stoic to the end, she ate a piece of the crusty bread and finished the soup before getting up. After putting her dishes away and wiping off the table, she went into the hallway. The atrium was lit with tiny spotlights that cast intriguing shadows on the walls.

The flicker of firelight came from the den. From the open door of his bedroom, a grandfather clock bonged out the time—seven o'clock. Early yet.

In the den, Rafe sat on the sofa with the throw pillows and an afghan. A lamp cast light onto the report he was reading. He barely glanced up when she entered and sat opposite him. She picked up a magazine on hotel management and started reading.

An hour passed.

"Would you like some hot cider?" he asked, laying the report on the lamp table.

"Yes." Her voice came out husky. She cleared her throat. "That would be nice. Can I help?"

"I can manage, thanks."

Stubborn. His father had been right to be worried about him. Rafe wasn't accepting anything from anyone.

He'd closed himself off after the funeral, but she thought time would have healed him, as it had her. It hadn't. He'd locked some essential part of himself away.

She remembered a song she'd heard when they'd eaten breakfast with a band of goatherds one morning. *I follow the wind/ Wild is the wind,* she'd translated the words, filled with unnamed longing. *And wild is my love for you,* she'd thought and looked at Rafe.

Genny woke with a start as a loud racket invaded her dreams. She listened intently and realized the noise must be a snowblower clearing out the winding paths to the town houses.

She wondered what the temperature was. The cold penetrated the room and her bed. Pulling the covers up until only her face peeked out didn't help. She was freezing.

The furnace must not be working. Or maybe something was wrong with the thermostat. She'd see if she could find it and—

A creaking of timber halted her thoughts.

She remembered she was supposed to be careful and alert. It was hard to think of danger when in the midst of paradise, though. The mountains were so beautiful with their covering of snow and trees. Every view was like a Christmas postcard.

After assuring herself it was only the wind making the house groan and whistle, she rose stealthily and slipped into her parka. She found the socks she'd taken off earlier, pulled them on her icy feet and slipped into a pair of soft moccasins.

She padded out onto the balcony. The atrium glowed with tiny spotlights—the living heart of the house. She touched the glass, wondering if the lights produced enough warmth to keep the plants from freezing. Apparently so.

A night-light lit the stairwell, and she had no trouble finding her way to the kitchen. She saw the luminous dial of the wall clock. Almost two.

Stopping, she listened to the roar of the snowblower coming closer. She slipped into the shadow of the stairwell and peered out the kitchen window.

The snow had stopped and a pale moon hung over the far mountain on the other side of the valley, giving the snow-covered landscape a surreal appearance. A streetlight gleamed through the pine woods between the road and the town houses.

On the path winding up the hill, a lone figure approached, a cloud of blowing snow preceding him as he guided the machine along the incline. He was a tall man, and large, made menacing by the added bulk of his winter clothing and the ski hat pulled over his face like a death mask. She wouldn't have been surprised to see two glowing coals where his eyes should have been.

Her heart leapt around in her chest, and she pressed a hand between her breasts to stifle the sensation. The hair prickled on the back of her neck.

Go with your instincts, her uncle had told her.

If she felt danger, then she was to assume danger was present. She watched the lone worker out in the snowy landscape, coming closer and closer. With the snowblower running, he could rush into the house, shoot them and be gone. No one would hear.

Light flooded the room.

She gave a startled gasp, almost a cry, and whirled. Rafe stood in the doorway, his hair ruffled from sleep, his jeans on and zipped, but with the snap unfastened. He wore no shirt or shoes.

"What's wrong?" he asked. His face showed no expression.

The noise stopped outside. She looked around. The snowblower was still on the path, but the worker had disappeared.

"Turn out the light," she ordered. She reached for the rocker switch by the back door and did it herself.

The worker appeared on the path near the steps. He raised his arms and crossed them over his head—a signal she recognized. It meant all was well.

"Oh," she said, relieved. With a half salute, the man turned away. In a minute, the blower started again.

"Who was that?" Rafe asked, crossing the room.

"My contact."

Rafe flipped on the kitchen lights again. "I suppose he's on my payroll. I should dock his salary for the lousy job he's been doing on the paths."

"He's very nice," she defended the agent, relieved to see him and know he was nearby. She realized his being one of the resort maintenance men gave him an excuse to be about at all hours. An excellent idea.

"Did the blower wake you up?" Rafe asked.

"Uh, yes," she said, recalling that it had. "But it was the cold that got me out of bed. I thought I'd check the thermostat. My bedroom is like the North Pole."

She glanced at his bare chest and wondered why he didn't have chill bumps. She did, and she wore a flannel gown and her parka along with socks and moccasins.

At that moment she became aware that Rafe, too, knew exactly what she wore. He perused her intently, taking in her tangled hair, her lack of makeup, her odd mix of clothing all the way to her feet. The light that blazed in his eyes told her he didn't find her dowdy or unattractive.

"I'm sorry," he said. "I like a cold room to sleep in. I try to remember to reset the thermostat when I have a...guest."

She wondered what word he'd thought to apply to her before he'd settled on guest. Intruder? Interloper?

He went to the control on the wall beside the atrium doorway and punched a new setting. She heard the click of the thermostat as it turned on the furnace.

"It should be warm soon."

"Thank you." She stood there for a second, gazing at him. There was a light furring over his chest, but not much. He wasn't a hairy man. She remembered how smooth his skin had felt under her hands when she'd caressed him.

She closed her eyes as yearning, so strong it was painful, swept over her. She'd wondered what her reaction to him would be, but she hadn't counted on this total lack of control around him. Her feelings simply took over and left no room for thinking and things like that.

She wished he'd take her to *his* bed.

Opening her eyes, she watched his gaze roam over her, back to her face. The first time they'd met, she'd thought he was the most attractive man she'd ever seen. Time hadn't altered that opinion.

He was staring at her mouth, she realized. Heat flowed into her lips, making them soft and puffy...ready for his kiss.

A whimper of need, low and husky, pushed its way from the back of her throat, startling her. Inside, she was all hard, tight emotion, stuffed into her skin until there was no room for the rest of her, no room for anything but him.

She wanted him . . . still.

The knowledge washed all other thoughts from her mind. She wanted to be close to him, to be held and loved, to make love and find the fulfillment she knew waited in his arms. They had almost shared that ecstasy once, but fate had intervened. Now . . . now there was another chance.

She lifted her arms, to gather him close to her and ease the ache she sensed they both felt.

He shuddered suddenly, then half turned from her and pressed a hand across his face.

"Rafe," she said, all shaky and hot and unsure. The wildness grew in her like the wind that preceded a storm. Her heart leapt in her chest, ready to follow that wanton calling.

Wild is the wind. Oh, yes!

Hands closed on her shoulders. "Stop it," he commanded. "Now. Stop it." He was angry at life, at her.

"I can't . . . help it," she confessed.

The need must have shown in her eyes. He cursed and released her. "Go back to your room."

She stood there, uncertain. Her heart urged her to stand her ground, to force him to acknowledge the passion and the need between them. But when he looked at her, it was with loathing.

Shocked, she stood there for a second. Pulling from his grip, she ran up the stairs to her room. She flung off her coat and shoes and leapt into the bed, shivering with emotions too turbulent to name.

* * *

Rafe threw off his jeans, but didn't climb back into bed. Instead he stood in the dark, letting the coldness of the room cool the raging heat in his blood.

His arousal was painful as his body defied the commands of his mind. No lessening of desire took place as he endured the cold. He doubted if lying in the snow would make a difference.

At once a picture of Genny came to him, lying under him on the desert sand, the ground cool in the shade of the many palm trees that lined the bubbling spring.

He'd followed her there, riding out on the fine-boned Arabian horse from the prize stable of the sheikh, feeling a need to watch over her when she headed for her favorite spot where the water leapt forth from a rocky outcropping only to disappear in the shining sands a few feet away.

He'd fallen under her spell so entirely he'd forgotten loyalty and friendship. He'd known only that he wanted her... for himself.

And she'd wanted him.

A groan pushed its way out of him. Defeated, he slipped into bed and let the memories gather and form and dissolve into others as they chose.

Genny. With her heavy fall of hair spread out over her shoulders, her eyes bright with interest while they'd talked. He hadn't meant to touch her, much less kiss her.

When he'd seen her ride out alone after the diplomatic meeting at which she'd acted as translator, he hadn't been able to resist going after her. He'd known Tom was in love with her and was trying to win her. But he'd also known she wasn't in love with Tom.

She'd been bending down to drink directly from the clear pool when he'd caught up with her. When she'd looked up, he'd lost the careful control he'd maintained around her for a month.

The cool water had dripped from her chin onto her white shirt. Sitting back on her heels, she'd laughed up at him and wiped the drops away with the back of her hand.

Remembering, his body surged with needs he could no longer fight. He pressed his arm over his eyes but that didn't block out the flow of images.

When the smile had faltered and left her face, he'd reached down and wiped the remaining drop of water off her bottom lip. And having touched her, he couldn't stop.

Ah, God, he *couldn't.*

He'd have died before he could have forced himself not to kneel down beside her, not to reach for her, not to cover that soft, sweet mouth with his.

She'd kissed him back, as generous with her passion as she was with her smiles. When he'd touched her breast, she'd caught her breath . . . then pushed against his hand, wanting more.

His hands shaking, he'd unbuttoned her blouse and removed the lacy covering. Hell, they were shaking now, he realized.

Flinging the covers aside, he went through the master bath and into the next room. With a flick of a switch, the cover lifted from the hot tub and the water began to froth and churn. He sank down into the spa and pulled a towel over for a headrest.

The rush of the water over his skin reminded him of the way she had run her hands over his torso in wonder, as if she'd just discovered the sense of touch that day. He knew how she'd felt. It had been the same for him—all new and wonderful and more powerful than anything he'd ever felt.

When he'd spread his shirt and laid her on it, she'd looked at him as if he were the only man in the world. She'd flipped her hair from under her so that it spread in dark shiny waves over the white cotton of his shirt, then she'd reached for him—

Standing abruptly, he stepped out of the hot tub, unlocked the side door and dived off the step into the snowbank.

"Is it time for the birch switches?" a sardonic male voice asked.

Chapter Three

Rafe, buried to his neck in the snow, grimaced. "Well, if it isn't the tooth fairy."

Deveraux walked up the steps, reached inside the door and grabbed a towel. He tossed it to Rafe, then peered at the hot tub. "I could go for that," he remarked. "I'm damn near frozen."

"Be my guest." Rafe stood and wrapped the towel around himself. He followed Deveraux inside and closed the door behind them.

"I haven't time," the undercover agent said regretfully.

"You got time for a chat?"

"Yeah."

"The kitchen's that way." Rafe pointed at the door. "I'll be out in a minute." He stepped into the shower, his mood dark. The powers-that-be wouldn't have assigned their best agent to the case if the situation wasn't perilous.

When he had showered and dressed, he went into the kitchen. The scent of hot chocolate filled the air. Genny was pouring it out. His outlook went darker.

"I found some chocolate-chip cookies," she said with a smile when he stopped at the end of the counter. "Have a seat."

He went to the table where Deveraux sat. Genny brought the three mugs to the table, then went back for a plate of cookies. When they were all seated, Rafe glanced from one to the other.

"You're probably wondering why I called this meeting," Deveraux quipped, dunking a cookie into the cocoa and downing it in two bites. He grinned at Genny.

Rafe noted that, like him, she wore jeans and a sweatshirt. Her hair was combed, and she'd put on a touch of lipstick. He looked away when she nibbled daintily on a cookie, then sipped her drink. His body perked up. He cursed silently.

"So start the meeting," he said curtly.

Genny reiterated her involvement. The agent outlined the plan, which was to lure the guy there and catch him.

"I've cleared the path to your back porch," Deveraux said. "Use that door for your comings and goings. The only tracks I want in the snow are mine or the guy we're after." He shot Rafe a warning glance. "No more Swedish baths."

Genny looked at Rafe with a question in her eyes.

He felt the heat in his neck and ears. Damn Deveraux for making him feel like an adolescent. "I'm glad you're on the case," he said, ignoring her. He'd worked with the special agent before. The man was an expert in the oil field, from pumping to selling. He was also a self-made millionaire. Impressive.

When the agent rose to leave, he paused and gazed from one to the other. "Glad you brought Genny here. It's the best possible place for her."

"I'm moving her to the lodge on Monday. The town house is too isolated—"

"We want her isolated," Deveraux interrupted. "Send her back to the chalet if you don't want her here. The lodge would make it harder to disguise the fact that we're keeping close tabs on her. I can't loiter about the corridors like a lovesick calf."

The two men locked eyes. Rafe finally heaved a sigh. "You're on," he said, as if agreeing to some unspoken pact.

The agent's smile flashed white against his deeply tanned skin. For a moment there was sympathy in his gaze, then he pulled his coat and gloves on. "One other thing. I'll wear a ski mask when I'm working outside at night. Just so you'll know it's me, I'll always have a green handkerchief tucked into this pocket with the end hanging out. Green, got that?"

Rafe nodded. So did Genny. He didn't look at her while he let Deveraux out, then locked the kitchen door. The light didn't come on automatically. Rafe waited until the other man was out of sight in the pine trees, then flicked the switch. The porch light came on. The automatic switch had been turned off, he realized.

Genny waited until Rafe turned back to her before speaking. "So I'm to stay here?" she asked, keeping her expression bland.

"Looks like it."

"But you don't want me," she reminded him.

Emotion flicked through his eyes, then was gone, but she saw pain and longing in that instant. Her insides went tight and hot and achy.

"I have a business to run. I told the spook house gang I wasn't going to play anymore almost three years ago. They seem unable to believe it."

"I'm sorry," she said, and meant it.

Rafe looked straight at her. "I see my father's hand in this. He wants me back. I'm not going. You can quote me on that next time you talk to him. Make him believe it, because it's a fact."

He walked out.

Genny poured the last dregs of cocoa into her cup and reheated it in the microwave oven. She turned out the light and sat in the dark, watching the play of moonlight and shadows on the deep drifts of fresh snow while she thought about the odd turns life could take.

The house was empty when she awoke the next morning. She peered at her watch through bleary eyes. Ten o'clock.

It was late, but she didn't want to get up. She didn't feel rested at all. Sighing, she forced herself from the warm cocoon, headed toward the bath, then stopped.

Her eyes narrowed as she ran a hand over the extra blanket that was now on her bed. It hadn't been there when she'd gone to sleep about four that morning. A flutter went through her.

She showered, then went to the kitchen when she was dressed.

A note on the oak table told her to stay in the house. Her host would return at noon with lunch. Since that was only a couple of hours away, she drank a glass of juice rather than eating.

Taking her coffee to the table, she picked up a section of the morning paper. Rafe had evidently read it earlier. Another pang fluttered through her chest. It felt right to be here. As if she belonged. The house welcomed her.

She made her bed and wandered through the place, straightening things, emptying the dishwasher when it finished its cycle, trying to stay busy. Finally, unable to curb her curiosity, she went to the master bedroom and peered in, not quite daring to enter.

It was a charming room of deep green and light tan. The king-size bed was neatly made and, other than a pair of jeans on the bedpost, no clothes cluttered the chairs. Rafe had such endearing domestic qualities. She'd never suspected.

The bathroom was to her left; beyond it was a room with a hot tub. A shiver of desire went through her at the image the intimate setting conjured. Lost in reverie, she was startled when the grandfather clock bonged twelve times.

Her pulse leapt into panic mode. It was time for Rafe to come home. She rushed back to the kitchen and settled on the padded bench to watch for his arrival. Soon she saw him coming up the path, a white bag in his hand.

She felt the way she had the day after they'd danced beside the garden wall that one time—filled with doubt and fear, yet tingly with excitement and an overpowering need to see him again.

The sun struck golden shafts of light off him and the snow. Everything, including her body, seemed new and strange to her, reacting in ways she couldn't control.

Their eyes met when he came up the steps, and she couldn't look away. He broke the connection and came to the door. Using a key, he unlocked the dead bolt and came inside, bringing the scent of the outdoors with him.

She inhaled deeply. "Mmm, you smell of pine and crisp winter air and..." She couldn't describe his masculine scent—shaving lotion and shampoo, soap and a clean, subtle aroma she couldn't name but one she associated with him.

He gave a slight snort and set the bag on the table. "Lunch."

"Good. I'm hungry." She chatted on about not waking until ten, then not eating when she found his note and realized he would soon be coming with lunch. "You added a blanket to my bed," she finally concluded. "Thanks."

"I realized I'd forgotten to tell you where extra ones were." He set two plastic thermal plates on the table and removed the lids. He poured himself a cup of coffee and offered to refill her cup. After he did so, they sat at the table, silent and stiff with each other.

"Am I going to stay here?" she finally asked.

"Is there a choice?"

"Yes. I don't mind going back to the chalet." She held her breath and waited for his answer.

He picked up a knife and fork and cut a piece of succulent roast beef. Broccoli and Yorkshire pudding accompanied the meal. "No, you'll stay where I can watch you. Another pair of eyes could make the difference between—" He stopped abruptly.

"Between life and death?"

"Don't you have enough sense to be afraid?" He spoke roughly. "These guys play for keeps, and they don't care who gets hurt." He paused, then repeated in a toneless voice, "They don't care."

"I know, but it's hard to face my own immortality," she mused aloud. "I can't imagine a person actually killing somebody else. It seems so..." She gestured helplessly.

"It's done all the time," he said, his tone callous and offhand, as if the thought didn't bother him at all.

She knew better. At one point during their desert assignment he'd been called away on an emergency trip. After rejoining them in the desert, his eyes had been bleak. "People died," he'd told her when they were alone and she'd gently but persistently probed into the cause. "Young boys who should have been in school, not packing guns."

That was when she'd realized the hidden depths in the man. It was probably the moment she'd started falling in love with him, although she'd been attracted from the first.

Genny sat there for a while before she began eating. The bleakness was back in his eyes. There, in the desert, as she'd come to know him, she'd found she wanted to bring laughter to his eyes, to make him enjoy life again.

For a while, she'd thought she had.

Then a terrorist had blown up the car he was supposed to have been in, and the light had blinked out like a candle in the wind. She suspected that incident had been the culmination of many.

Looking at him now, she felt a chill creep over her. He was so withdrawn and cold, she might never reach him again.

No, she refused to accept that. She could be here for days...weeks...months. There was time. And she was not without a certain amount of stubbornness herself.

"I have to get back to the office," he announced.

"Mmm." She'd expected as much, but she was disappointed all the same. "I think I'll take a walk."

"No."

"Rafe—"

"You're not to go out without me or Deveraux with you. That's final, so don't bother arguing. Give me too much trouble and I'll call your uncle."

She sighed and subsided. Her uncle had urged her to come to the resort. He'd felt she would be safer there. He'd also noticed her interest in Rafe. So had Rafe's father. Too bad the son wasn't as clear-eyed.

Well, maybe not. She wasn't sure she wanted Rafe to be able to read her every thought. He could see into her much too much for her comfort already.

"What time will you be home?" she asked.

He hesitated, then gave her a cynical smile. "Are you going to have my supper and slippers waiting?"

"Sorry. I didn't mean to come across as the little woman," she answered just as coolly. "I just wondered how many hours I was going to have to stay cooped up by myself."

He planted his hands on his hips and frowned thoughtfully at her. "I'll see what I can do," he promised and, grabbing his parka, slung it on and went out. He stood on the porch and gave her a severe glare until she came over and clicked the dead bolt into place. Then he left.

Rafe met the agent on the path through the trees. "She's antsy, wants to go out for a walk. I told her not to go anywhere unless one of us was with her."

Deveraux frowned and said, "Hmm."

"I want you to stay around the town houses. I'll tell Bill that I've assigned you to work up there."

"Hmm."

"In fact, you can do some work in the town house, maybe paint it—"

"Hmm," Deveraux interrupted.

"Is that all you can say?" Rafe demanded.

"No," he said pleasantly. "First, I'm the field commander on this case, not you. Second, no one paints in zero-degree weather. Third, quit hovering over her like a hen with one chick. How are we going to draw the guy out if she's never available?"

Rafe grabbed the agent by the lapels of his coat. "Dammit, you're not going to set her up like a clay pigeon. This is her *life* you're playing with."

"Ease off, Barrett. We have everything under control—"

"We?" Rafe let go of the coat and stepped back.

"According to a reliable contact, our man arrived in New York last night. He's apparently altered his appearance."

A chill settled painfully in Rafe's chest. The assassin was in the States. That information made the menace seem that much closer to Genny. Rafe wanted to grab her and run . . . just run. . . .

"The local police are cooperating with us," Deveraux finished, "so you can ease up on the watchdog act."

"Yeah, right," Rafe said. He glanced at his watch. "I have an appointment in a few minutes." He strode down the trail.

A picture of Genny came to him. She was riding a dun-colored Arabian mare, dressed in a blue shirt and tan slacks. Her dark hair flicked behind her as she raced across the sand, her laughter trailing her. She was like a chimera, a desert phantom he'd never hoped to catch.

But he had caught her. And touched her. And kissed her.

He let his breath out explosively, and a cloud of steam plumed in front of him. He had to quit remembering those days. As soon as it was safe, she'd leave, and his life would be peaceful again.

Peaceful or empty? a part of him questioned.

He swore to himself and hurried on to the office.

Rafe jogged along the path. It was past six and dark in the woods, but the way was lighted by foot lamps along the trail. He noticed one of them was out and made a note to tell Deveraux to get it replaced.

He was later than he'd meant to be. At the last minute he'd had a call from a supplier and had been tied up on that for more than an hour. Genny was probably climbing the walls with boredom, but he'd make it up to her. He'd take her out to dinner.

The porch light was on when he reached the town house. He ran up the steps and stopped at the kitchen door, his heart thudding.

Genny was inside. She was peering into a pot on the stove. The oak table was set with place mats and dinner plates.

He stood there, watching her, unable to move. A painful longing pierced his chest. To have her waiting when he came home... To make a home with her...

He shoved the thought aside. The domestic scene conjured up ideas he wanted to act upon, like taking her to his bed and keeping her there until morning. He reached for the door.

She looked up when the door rattled. It was locked, he noted, pleased that she'd obeyed him in this. Before he could retrieve the key from his pocket, she flew across the room.

"Come in," she said with a big smile. "Supper is almost ready. Your secretary said—"

"I don't have a secretary," he snapped.

"Oh. Well, your assistant, then. Valerie? Is that her name?"

He nodded as he crossed to the stairwell and tossed his parka over the newel. Sitting on the steps, he removed his boots.

"Anyway, she called and said you'd probably be another hour. If you're hungry, we can eat."

She seemed almost breathless when she finished. Her glance was a tad defiant. He thought of other ways to make her breath leave her. He knew where to stroke her to make her purr.

Enough of those thoughts!

Her green sweatshirt matched the color of her eyes. Her hair was pulled back with a headband. She wore no makeup that he could detect. She looked young and earnest as she peered into a boiling pot. He looked away.

The aroma of food set his mouth to watering. He realized he was hungry. He rose and stretched, then padded off to his bedroom to wash up. When he came back, the meal was on the table.

"Chicken and dumplings," he said. "I haven't had anything like that since my grandmother retired to Florida, quit cooking and started playing bingo."

Genny laughed. She filled their coffee cups, then took the chair opposite his. He sat down and picked up his napkin.

"You look thoughtful," she said.

"The assassin arrived in New York yesterday."

Genny caught her breath at the bluntness of the statement. Fear had her clutching her hands together. "Mad Dog," she said.

"What?"

"That's what he's called. His business nom de plume, so to speak." Actually, it was the code name of this operation. If Rafe heard the man's name, he'd realize he was in danger, too.

"Mad Dog," he repeated, his hard gaze on her, his thoughts unreadable. Still watching her, he picked up his fork and started eating the food she'd prepared.

"Where did you get all this?" he asked after a minute, indicating the vegetables, bread and casserole.

"My other guardian angel went to the store."

"Deveraux." Rafe frowned. "I told him to stay up here. The store is half a mile away. Some guardian he is, going off and leaving you unprotected."

She glanced upward in exasperation, then grinned impudently at him. "I feel safe enough with two angels watching over me."

He gave her an assessing perusal. "I'm no angel."

Her blood heated as he let his mask of indifference slip for a second. "You're named after one. Rafael, an archangel. The agent's name is Gabriel, another archangel, the messenger of God."

"Or death," Rafe reminded her. "Deveraux was the one who told me about the killer."

Genny stubbornly stuck with her original line of thought. "Rafael in Hebrew means 'God has healed,' but I wonder..."

Rafe gave her a dark scowl. "You wonder what?"

"If you've healed," she said, bringing the subject to light hesitantly. "You were...wounded...when Tom died." She waited, wanting him to explain why he'd cut her out of his life.

A muscle moved in the side of his jaw. "That's in the past. I've forgotten it."

"I don't think so."

He pushed his chair back savagely. It made a protesting squeal against the slate flooring. "I don't know what you're trying to do, but stay out of my psyche. If this is a plot by my father to get me back into the corps, it won't work, however much I might be tempted by you." His leer was deliberate and mocking.

"I'm not... I didn't mean..." But she was talking to empty air. She heard his bedroom door slam a second later.

She picked up her fork, but her hand trembled too much for her to eat. Filled with remorse for probing where she had no business, she cleared the table, put the food away and cleaned the kitchen.

Going into the den, she added wood to the fire she'd started earlier and sat on the sofa, her feet drawn up under her. Rafe wanted her, but he also hated her. *Why?*

An hour later he came into the room. She looked up from the book she was reading. "I'm not here because your father wanted me to lure you back into service," she quickly stated. "I chose to come because I wanted to see you again."

"I thought you needed a safe place," he challenged.

She gazed into the fire, aware of the unknown dangers surrounding them. "I do." A wry smile flickered across her lips and died. "But I'm not so sure this is one."

The crackling of the flames seemed loud in the silence. She risked a glance at him. The bleakness was back in his eyes. It startled her. Then he smiled cynically. "You're probably right. People who hang around me tend to come to bad ends."

"I wasn't referring to that kind of danger." She faced him and slowly, cautiously, let him see inside her.

Their eyes locked. The tension built. She could almost hear it humming in the air between them. A shiver went over her. She felt suddenly alone and afraid as his eyes grew colder.

Let me in, she wanted to say. *It's lonely out here.* But she didn't. At last, with a defeated sigh, she turned to the fire and drew its warmth into her.

"I'm hungry," he said after a while. "We didn't eat the dinner you fixed." He rose and headed for the kitchen.

She followed.

He set the bowls out and handed her a plate. They loaded up and heated the food in the microwave oven.

When they were seated at the table, she said, "Rafe, we have to talk."

"Not tonight. Let's pretend, instead."

"Pretend?"

"That we just met. That we're two ordinary people with no past between us." His tone challenged her to accept his rules.

"Can we do that?" she questioned in a low tone of doubt.

"Yes," he said harshly. He took a bite of food. "This is very good. Did your mother teach you to cook?"

Genny followed his lead. "Not really. She doesn't like anyone to get in her way when she's in the kitchen. I've taken lessons, both in the States and in France. Tomorrow I thought I'd make bean soup from a recipe I got at an inn near Nice."

They discussed foods they'd tried in various parts of the world while they lingered over the meal. Later they returned to the den with coffee and apple pie—a frozen one she'd baked earlier. The bonging of the clock at ten made her realize they'd been talking for hours.

She smiled at him contentedly. "We used to talk like this," she murmured. "There in the desert—"

He looked away from her, but not before she'd seen the raw, naked pain tear across his face. For a second the bones seemed to stand out as if his skin had been drawn tight. Then it was gone, so fast she wasn't sure she'd seen it.

"Tell me what thought just occurred to you."

He laughed harshly. "You wouldn't want to know."

"I do."

"Then you're a fool."

A sense of helplessness hit her. His father had been right. Something had happened to Rafe inside.

He rose and stoked the fire, which already burned brightly. The light made his white shirt translucent, and she could see the outline of his strong torso through it. The muscles rippled under the cloth as he bent forward to add a log to the grate.

"I've missed you," she whispered, caught in the despair of his unexplained rejection. "Three years is a long time."

He made a sound deep in his throat.

"Why didn't you ever come back?" she asked, remembering the long months in Paris after the tragedy. "I needed you."

"I had nothing to give you." He spoke without inflection, as if all life had fled.

She swooped down beside him. Tentatively, she laid a hand on his upper arm. "We could have comforted each other."

Again she caught a glimpse of some deep, terrible anguish in him, and shuddered in reaction. "Like this?" he asked. With a cruel twist to his lips, he bent to her.

The kiss was hard and unforgiving. She tried to draw back, but he caught her head in his cupped hands and held it in a vise. His mouth ground against her, closed and hard. The kiss ended as abruptly as it began.

He thrust her away and stood over her. "Was that comforting enough?" he demanded hoarsely.

She shook her head, wanting to flee, wishing she hadn't started this. "Why are you angry with me?"

Turning away, he paced the room. "I'm not angry with you."

"You're angry about something." When he said nothing, she spoke again. "There in the desert...I thought we were falling in love."

His hands clenched into fists. "And what about Tom? What did you think about him, or did you think of him at all when we were wallowing around in the sand and he took a hit that was intended for me?"

Chapter Four

Genny stared up at Rafe, seeing the anger and loathing in his eyes in the second before he left. His words made no sense. She followed him to his room.

"What about Tom?" she asked, trying to understand.

He stood by the window, looking out at the night. He whirled and faced her. "Leave it. It doesn't matter now."

There was a look of untamed ferocity about him, like that of a beast who had run as far as he could and had no choice but to make one last, desperate stand.

"No," she said, unafraid. "I want to know exactly what you meant by that remark about Tom."

"It's obvious. I should have gone into town and met the diplomat at the airport. There would have been time after the meeting. If I'd done my duty, Tom wouldn't have died. If I'd gone, things might have been different."

She shook her head, still puzzled. "No one knew of the bomb."

"*I* should have. It was my operation. I should have known there was danger. I should have suspected it, prepared for it."

"But no one did," she reminded him. An ache started within her. "Why are strong men so hard on themselves?" she asked.

"Strong?" He laughed without mirth. "Don't you get it? I wanted to be with you. That's why I didn't go."

A light dawned in her. "You... you blame me."

"No!" He reached out as if to reassure her, then drew back. "But I was glad when Tom volunteered."

"The choice was his. He broke his promise to ride with me so he could go. He thought it might further his career. Tom was very ambitious," she pointed out to him.

"Don't you think I knew that?" Rafe's smile was as brittle as glass. "When he suggested he should meet the diplomat at the airport—in case the meeting went on longer than planned—I didn't argue. But I knew the meeting would be over on time." His glare challenged her to deny the statement.

She couldn't.

"I should have been the one in the car," he concluded with a grimness that wrenched at her heart.

"You couldn't have known what would happen," Genny reminded him sympathetically. "You can't blame yourself—"

He crossed the room until he stood no more than three feet from her. "Can't I?" he asked with deadly quiet. "I let myself be distracted from my responsibilities. I wasn't there to frolic in the sand, but to do a job. I failed—"

"You didn't!" Feeling the coldness emanating from him, she wrapped her arms across her chest.

"I let...things get in the way." His voice was harsh. "I wanted you like hell. From the first moment. I still do."

"Is that so terrible?" Her voice trembled, and she fought to control it, feeling she was close to understanding him.

"It is when it makes a man forget who he is and what he's supposed to be doing," he told her in a voice as barren as a snow-swept plain. "You're a weakness I can't afford." He walked into the adjoining bath and closed the door.

She blinked as if struck. The soft click was like the slam of a gate, a barrier to the future.

Rafe was reading the Sunday paper when she went into the kitchen the next morning. "Poached eggs and bacon in the oven," he said with hardly a glance her way.

"Thanks." She fixed toast and poured a cup of coffee.

She ate, read the front section of the paper, then got up, went over to the bench and sat in the corner, watching tiny flakes of snow drift past the window. She sighed and leaned her head against the glass, feeling subdued and introspective.

"Do you ski?" he asked.

She studied his expression before answering. "Yes."

"There's rental equipment at the lodge. We can try out the slopes if you'd like."

"You sound as if you'd enjoy that about as much as leaping in front of an avalanche." She managed a smile.

He shrugged. "I figure if I don't get you outside, you'll take off on your own and end up in trouble."

"Thanks for the vote of confidence."

"Do you want to go or not?" he demanded impatiently.

She couldn't read his mood. "I'm strictly an intermediate."

"We'll stick to the easy slopes."

"I guess it'll be all right."

His frown deepened at her lack of display of enthusiasm. What did he expect from her? That she'd jump for joy when he'd made it obvious he didn't want her on the same continent with him?

"Let's see what clothes you have." He stood and waited for her to precede him up the stairs.

He lounged against the frame of her door and approved her jeans and nylon powder pants, the turtleneck pullover and wool sweater that would be worn under her parka.

"What about underwear?" he asked.

"I'm wearing a bra," she said defensively.

His glance dipped downward, then back up to her face. A flicker of a smile suddenly appeared at the corners of his mouth, then was gone. "I meant, *long* underwear. It's damn cold out there today, two degrees below zero."

"I don't have any."

"I'll see what I can do." He swung around and strode off. In a minute he was back. He tossed a bundle onto her bed. "Try those on. They shrunk in the dryer and are too short for me. See if you can get your pants on over them." He left.

She closed the door before shedding her outer clothing. Pulling on his long johns seemed much too intimate. It was almost like being surrounded by him, with every inch of her being caressed at the same time.

A tremor of longing raced through her. How could she find the man who'd once warmed her very core in this icy stranger who allowed no one to come close?

Rafe watched Genny push off down the slope. She was a little wobbly, but her form was good. They'd been skiing for almost three hours. One more run, he decided, then they'd call it a day. She was getting tired, and her skiing showed it.

He glanced at the people getting off the chair lift. It was early yet and not crowded. The afternoon would be busier when half-day tickets went on sale. He and Genny had made about fifteen runs that morning. Maybe she'd be content to stay in the town house the rest of the day. And the rest of the week.

He felt invaded by her presence, but for now he was stuck with her. As soon as it was safe, he'd send her packing.

When she stopped, he let his skis head down the hill. In a minute, he skidded to a halt beside her in a smooth side slip, throwing up a small spray of snow as he did.

"I'd forgotten how much fun this is," she exclaimed. "Do you know this is the first time I've skied in the States. When I was in Paris, I used to go to the Alps quite a bit."

He glanced away from her pink cheeks and sparkling eyes, refusing to respond to her gaiety. "Are you warm enough?"

"Yes, the long johns are super, except for being a little bunched up in the waist. Thanks for loaning them to me."

She pushed off, but he stayed for a second. The thought of her in his clothing wreaked havoc on his libido. He went into full arousal. Fortunately, his powder bibs hid the fact.

Forcing his mind to other things, he looked around and realized they were the only ones who'd taken this particular side run through the woods. The rest of the early bird skiers had taken off on the rolling slope under the ski chair.

Damn. He should have taken Genny that way, too. She'd be safer in a group. He took off after her. Just as he came alongside her, she caught an edge and lost her balance.

He swerved sharply, but too late. She hit his thigh in her fall, knocking his ski out from under him. They went down in a tumble of arms, legs, poles and skis.

The slope in this section was steep and pitched to the east, toward a grove of fir trees. Rafe realized they were aiming right for the trees and the deep powder, which could be hellacious to climb out of. He grabbed Genny against him and dug in his heels.

Too late. They fell into the well of soft snow at the base of a huge fir.

He lay there on his back for a stunned minute, his head pointing down, Genny sprawled all over him. For another second, he let himself drift, savoring the feel of her body on his, then he realized she wasn't moving.

"Genny?"

She gave a choked sound.

"Are you all right? Genny? Answer me, dammit!" He reached for her head, but hesitated to move her in case she was seriously injured. His heart went into overtime. "Genny?"

She shook her head and pushed up on her arm. He got a glimpse of green eyes and a snow-covered face; then her arm sank into the soft snow and she disappeared again.

"*Mummff, mummff, mummff,*" she said.

He slipped his hands under her shoulders and lifted her so she rested on him, her face clear of the snow.

She used his chest as a base to push herself upright. When she blinked, snow tumbled down her cheeks in a small avalanche. She shook her head, causing a small flurry.

He felt himself sink farther into the drift. "We're in for it now. We'll have a hell of a time crawling out of here."

"I'm freezing," she said.

Relieved that she was okay, he allowed himself to relax. "You have snow all the way down your neck to your navel, most likely," he said, trying for a coolness he didn't feel. He assessed the situation. "I'm sinking toward China. You'll have to climb off."

She rubbed the rest of the snow out of her eyes and glanced around. A groan tore out of her when she saw how far it was up to the ski trail.

"Roll off," he ordered. "I'll dig out the skis and toss them up to you when you get back on the groomed stuff."

Instead of rolling, she tried to stand up. Her leg sank out of sight to her hip. "I'm stuck."

"Haven't you ever been in deep powder before?"

"Not *this* deep. Normally I stay on the ski run, except when hotdoggers run over me." She glared at him.

"If that isn't just like a woman," he complained, but not very fiercely. He'd slipped downward until his back rested against the tree. She was wedged against him. Her hips fit cozily into the niche between his legs. "*I* wasn't the cause of this fiasco."

"And *I* was?" She put both hands in the middle of his chest and pushed herself up. That had the effect of pressing her lower body much more tightly to his. The thrashing of her legs as she tried to free them from the snow caused sensations of desire to explode in him.

He slid his hands down her and clasped her hips. "Be still," he said in a strained voice.

She stopped pushing against him.

He hadn't had a woman in so long, he thought he'd forgotten what that part of his body was for. Being around her reminded him that he hadn't.

Closing his eyes, he held her there...just for a minute...just until he could catch his breath and get everything under control. One move, and it would be all over for him.

He knew the moment she became aware of his predicament. She went very still, then let her head fall back down on his chest.

"You feel good." He hadn't meant to say it, but the truth tumbled out of him unbidden. It had always been that way when he was with her. He bared his soul.

She stirred finally and tried to ease away.

Ah, God help him, but he couldn't let her go. "Don't," he whispered, his voice hoarse with need. The cold was all around them, but where she touched him, he was warm...on fire.

After an eternity, he released her and drew a deep breath. "You'll have to roll off me," he instructed her, "then swim like a frog uphill to get out of here. Understand?"

She nodded against his chest. She rolled to his side, then rolled again until she was on her stomach in the snow, her head upslope of them. She found her ski poles and held on to them as she began squirming up the deep drift with her arms and legs to the sides, using froggy strokes as he'd told her.

At one point, she had to stop and rest. He could hear her panting with the effort to flounder her way through the snow. At last, she made it to the packed snow of the run.

"I made it," she called back. "I've found one ski. Mine, I think. Yes, and here's the other."

"Good. I'll try to find mine and throw them up to you." He searched around in the snow, his arms going in up to his armpits. He found the errant skis and tossed them up to her, then crawled out on his stomach, using the same strokes she had.

When he reached the packed snow, he turned over on his back and stared at the sky while he rested.

"That could be dangerous," she said. She sat with one leg drawn up, her wrists crossed over her knee and her cheek resting on the back of her right hand.

"Yeah, snow can be a killer."

She leaned over him suddenly and laid a gloved hand over his mouth. "Don't. Let's just be a couple up here for the weekend. No cares. No worries. No thoughts of anything but now." She removed her hand.

Pushing himself up, he touched her under her chin. When she turned fully toward him, he brushed the snow off her bangs and knit hat; then he let his gloved fingers trail down her face until he could cup her chin again. He bent toward her. She didn't move.

Her lips were soft, warm, sensual under his. They fed the fire that blazed within him until he was consumed by it.

All rational thinking stopped. He knew the moment her arms came around him, but not when the sun disappeared behind a cloud. He knew the moment her mouth opened under his, but not when the snow started falling again.

He slid his tongue inside her mouth and felt the welcoming stroke of hers. The need overcame all else. He pressed her back.

"Rafe, no," she whispered. "We mustn't. We can't. Not here. Not now."

He frowned when she tried to draw away. Slowly her words penetrated the haze of passion that surrounded his senses.

A sense of déjà vu overcame him. "You said that before," he muttered, then remembered when and where.

"The desert," she said, confirming the memory. She smiled at him, and it was filled with regret.

He looked around quickly, feeling the prickle of danger on his neck. "Some guard I am." He helped her to her feet and got her back in the skis. He had an urgent feeling that he needed to get her back to civilization before it was too late, mainly because of the situation between them rather than any outside danger.

When they were both ready, he told her to go ahead. "Stick close to the middle of the run. Stay alert."

Genny noted the tone of urgency in him. He was worried about her all of a sudden. He'd gone from raging desire to cool control without a blink between.

A shudder went through her. If there was danger, they needed to get back to safety. Forgetting to think of her every move, she skied fast and clean.

Rafe stayed close behind her, dogging her every turn. Soon they reached the lodge where she returned her rental equipment. "Hot chocolate?" he asked. His smile was guarded, his libido under wraps once more.

She was disappointed. For a few minutes, they'd been close, mentally, not just physically. She wanted it again.

"At the house," she suggested. "I'll even volunteer to make it and clean up the pan afterward."

"If you use the microwave, you don't mess up a pan."

"Oh, yes, I forget these modern conveniences." She laughed and was pleasantly surprised when he did, too. In a few minutes, trudging back to the town house beside him, she stole several glances at him, wondering about that episode on the slope.

He paused on the path. "I'm not immune to your body, especially when it's glued to mine like tape to paper, but that's all there was to that moment on the slope. Don't try to read more into it."

* * *

Genny looked at the plants in the atrium, then ambled into the living room. Here the color scheme was dominated by the warmer tones of a deep golden beige carpet. The sofa was a jacquard print in subtle tones of sienna and turquoise. The north wall was fieldstone with an enormous fireplace. The windows were in the side walls. She stood and looked out at the snow.

After a few minutes, she returned to her favorite place—the cushioned bench in the kitchen. Settling in the corner with her back to the wall, she stretched out her legs and winced.

She was already getting sore from her strenuous exercise that morning. She shouldn't have skied for three hours straight.

Hmm, maybe that was Rafe's plan—to make her so sore she couldn't move for a week.

He'd left her at the town house after lunch at the lodge, which had been unbelievably crowded, and returned to his office to do some work. That had been three hours ago.

Work, ha! He'd wanted to get away from her.

A sigh escaped her. She watched the family next door spill out of their car. The parents gathered various belongings while the two boys tossed snowballs at each other over the car roof. When their father spoke to them, they stopped the horseplay and helped carry skis and poles inside.

A couple wandered up the path hand in hand. She wondered if they were honeymooners. Through the pines, she could see several cars on the main road.

She wanted to get out into the crisp air and— Why not? This was silly. It wasn't as if some madman was going to jump out from behind a bush and grab her in broad daylight. There was no reason not to go for a walk and work some kinks out.

Except that Rafe would probably give her a tongue-lashing if he caught her out alone.

That thought produced another. She paused, savoring the memory of his lips on hers, his tongue stroking inside her mouth, tasting her and tempting her into an answering passion.

Against her bra, her nipples contracted painfully. She wanted more than memories, she admitted, feeling the excitement beat through her. She wanted . . . Maybe she'd better go for that walk.

Donning her parka and knit cap with the red tassel, she walked out onto the porch and breathed in the cold air like a person just freed from prison. Jogging down the steps, she zipped the jacket and set out along the cleared flagstone path across the grassy meadow.

The sun tried to peek out of the cloud layer, but only a few feeble rays streaked through to the west of the resort. A light snow was still falling.

In the woods, she noticed the trail lamps had come on. The day was fast fading into twilight as the clouds thickened. The sound of the falling snow was louder.

An eerie sensation crept over her, sending goose bumps spiraling down her neck, as if someone had put a snowball down her shirt. Honestly, she was becoming paranoid. There were people on the road below her and at the town houses above her.

She stopped and glanced all around, as if surveying the beauty of the scenery. She was the only person in sight. A thrill of fear raced over her nerves.

Cool it, she chided. She could hear the shouts of the two boys, who'd come outside to play in the snow again.

The low hum of car engines came from the road. Civilization surrounded her.

She was only going to walk to the main lodge and surprise Rafe. Maybe he'd quit work and walk back with her. Anyway, she could hang around in the restaurant for a while and at least *see* some people, even if she didn't have anyone to talk to.

She started down the path and came out on the paved road that wound down the mountain to the highway twenty-six miles away. She paused to let a car pass, then continued across and down the path again. Here the land was steeper and railroad-tie steps had been put in the trail.

Halfway down, the trail opened into another meadow, much smaller than the one in front of the town houses, narrow but long.

A motion in the trees a hundred yards to her right caught her eye. Her chest squeezed tight when she spied a man there...a large man, beckoning to her to come to him.

She froze.

The man waved, then beckoned for her.

At last, her mind started functioning. "Oh, Deveraux," she murmured aloud, as if reassuring herself.

The man wore a knit mask over his face. He had a toboggan cap over that. His parka was dark green with light splashes, a sort of camouflage jacket.

She took a step off the path. The snow went right over her high-top hiking boots and up to her knees. Why didn't he come to her if they needed to talk?

Pulling back, she stepped on the path again and looked at the agent in frustration. He beckoned once more, impatiently this time. She huffed out a breath and gingerly stepped into the snow.

Snow can be a killer.

She recalled Rafe's sardonic remark when they'd worked their way out of the tree well. She hesitated as fear loomed like a specter in her, then shook her head. She was being ridiculous.

And yet . . .

All at once, she leapt back as if stung. *Handkerchief.* There was no green handkerchief—no handkerchief of any kind—dangling from the man's pocket!

She glanced wildly around, heart pounding. When she looked back at the woods, the man had disappeared. She blinked, then reacted instinctively. She ran for dear life.

The frightfully cold wind caused tears to collect at the corners of her eyes as she raced blindly along the trail. She wanted to escape the woods before an icy hand grabbed the back of her neck, halting her in her tracks.

Nothing stopped her. She careened into the Y where the trail met the lodge walkway, the place where she'd run into Rafe two days ago. She wished it would happen again, but she didn't meet up with him until she was almost at the lodge. She saw him coming down the broad steps and rushed toward him.

When he heard her steps, he glanced up. She saw surprise light his face for a second, then she threw herself into his arms.

"What is it? What's wrong? Are you hurt?"

The reassuring gruffness of his voice, filled with concern, almost broke her composure. She held on to it and to him with the grim determination of a bulldog.

"Are you hurt?" he demanded, more forcefully this time.

"No," she gasped. She gulped in several breaths and calmed her quaking nerves. Some Mata Hari she was, afraid of a shadow in the woods.

"What is it?" His face darkened. "What are you doing out by yourself? Where's Deveraux?"

"I don't know." She lifted her face from where she'd buried it against his neck and inhaled the wonderfully male fragrance that came from him.

He must have seen the remnants of fear in her eyes. When he spoke, it was on a gentler note. "What frightened you?"

"I... nothing. A shadow. Perhaps a deer."

"Where?"

"In the woods." She looked behind her. A shudder went through her. Had she seen someone? "I think it was just an overactive imagination." She managed a shaky laugh.

He was quiet for a moment, obviously thinking. Then he took her hand and led her into the lodge and to the restaurant.

"Bring a pot of hot tea," he said to the waitress, "then a full English tea after that."

"Yes, sir." The woman rushed off.

At a booth, located so they couldn't be seen from the entrance or the wide expanse of windows, he pushed Genny onto a banquette and sat down beside her.

When the tea arrived, he poured her a cup, added sugar and cream, tasted it, then held it to her lips. "Drink this."

It wasn't until she'd finished the cup and he'd poured her another that he spoke again. "Tell me exactly what happened." There was an air of controlled danger about him.

She felt utterly ridiculous. "I think I made a fool out of myself." She grimaced, then smiled ruefully.

He didn't return the smile. "Better a fool than a corpse."

"Well, you have a point," she conceded. "Really, it was nothing. I thought I saw a man. Actually I thought it was Gabriel Deveraux beckoning to me from the woods."

She told him the tale, realizing how fanciful it sounded now. "I'm sure I must have been mistaken—"

"How was he dressed?"

A flush heated her cheeks. "In the dark and light green parka he had on the other night. Also the ski mask and black knit cap. I'd actually taken a couple of steps toward him—it . . . whatever—when I realized there was no handkerchief. I panicked and ran."

"Thank God," Rafe muttered. "That's the one sensible thing you did. Why did you leave the damn house?"

"Well, I was bored and . . . and lonely."

His glare was ferocious. Fortunately the waitress arrived with pound cake, scones, clotted cream, whipped cream, assorted jellies and jams and sliced strawberries. He subsided without saying anything until the food was set out.

"Thanks," he said to the young woman, who nodded and left at once. He turned back to Genny. "Eat. You need to replace the blood sugar you used up when you ran."

His expression was still fierce, but his tone was oddly patient. She cast him a grateful smile. He ate little of the luscious food while she, after a bite of scone, stuffed herself.

"Can we get a doggie bag?" she asked, eyeing the rest of the goodies when she could hold no more.

A smile almost curled his mouth.

"Watch it," she advised. "If you smile, the world will stand still and we'll all fall off."

"Very funny." He got up, went into the kitchen and returned. "Here." He handed her a white, waxed bag.

When she had the rest of the scones and cake packed, he took her arm and pulled her to her feet.

"Oh-hh," she groaned. "I won't be able to walk tomorrow."

This time he was mockingly amused. "Good. Maybe you'll stay put if you're too sore to move."

"I thought that was the diabolical plot you'd hatched."

They walked along the path. The snow fell steadily. The sky seemed to darken with each step. She noticed Rafe kept a sharp watch all around without being obvious about it.

When she slipped, he caught her hand and placed it in the crook of his arm. She felt something too hard to be flesh under his parka. A holster, she realized. A gun and holster.

Life seemed terribly vulnerable all at once. She tightened her grip on his arm and stayed close.

At his home, he opened the door and let her go in first. "Here," he said. "You'd better keep this on you." Reaching up over the door trim, he removed an object.

She caught the key when he tossed it to her. "Thanks."

After placing the bag on the counter and hanging her jacket and hat on the newel, she shook out her hair, then stretched with a creaking of joints and a protest from her muscles. She groaned loudly.

"You want to use the hot tub?"

She glanced up at him from her seat on the steps. She finished unlacing her boots and tugged them off. "That would be nice."

"I'll show you how it works."

She followed him into his room, through the master bath and into the spa room. He flipped the switch to lift the cover and start the whirlpool jets. "Here's the timer.

Fifteen minutes is all that's recommended. You don't have any blood pressure problems, do you?''

Only when you're around. ''No,'' she said. He put the timer on. ''Towels,'' he pointed out. A stack of huge, fluffy ones were within arm's reach of the hot tub.

After glancing around, he went out.

Genny stood there beside the bubbling cauldron for a second, wondering if she should go upstairs and put on her bathing suit. She decided she didn't need it. Once she'd stripped out of her clothes, she stuck a toe, then a foot, into the water.

It was heavenly. She eased all the way down into the spa. The seat was the perfect height so all of her was covered right up to her neck. Using a towel for a headrest, she closed her eyes and let all the tension of the past hour drain out of her system.

When the timer went off, she couldn't bring herself to move. The water kept churning, so she saw no reason to try. She'd stay five more minutes.

Rafe glanced at his watch, then at the clock over the mantel in the den. It had been more than twenty minutes. He hadn't heard Genny come out of his room. With his luck, she'd probably gone to sleep in there. He'd have to see about her before she drowned.

A flicker of pain hit him, then was gone. Nothing was going to happen to her. He'd see to that if it was the last thing he did. He wouldn't allow her to be hurt.

For a second, the wall he kept around his emotions wavered. Nothing had changed simply because she was here, he reminded himself savagely. He'd never again let desire for her get in the way of duty. He'd stay in control from now on.

He strode through his quarters and into the spa room.

Just as he'd thought. She'd gone to sleep, her head cushioned on a towel and turned slightly to one side.

The water swirled around her body, giving him tantalizing glimpses of pink flesh without affording a clear-cut view of what he was looking at.

It didn't matter. His imagination supplied the details.

Her hair was spread out on the beige towel, except for one lock that had fallen into the water. The force of the jets made the curl dance in front of her breast.

Before he thought, he stooped and lifted the strand out of the water. For a heartbeat of time, he glimpsed the perfect, pink globe just below the water's surface, then the bubbles obscured the treasure again.

He swallowed hard against the desire that throbbed into instant life within. Why her? he wondered. Why not any one of a dozen beautiful women he met in the course of a day at the resort? From the moment they'd met, he thought only of her.

Dropping the curl, he cursed silently, then spoke. "Okay, dream girl, back to grim reality. It's time to get out."

She opened her eyes with a languid air. Her lashes were clumped together with moisture, and her skin had flushed with the heat of the whirling water. Her mouth tempted him, moist and pink and sort of puffy, as if she'd already been kissed.

She looked beautiful and desirable in every way a man could dream of. He'd dreamed about her a lot.

He told himself to get up, to leave.

He didn't.

He told himself she was just another woman.

She wasn't.

When she smiled at him, he couldn't fight the temptation. He reached for her.

Chapter Five

Genny stayed utterly still. She watched his gaze sweep over her, going from her eyes to her mouth... lingering there... then dropping lower. She glanced down.

The water concealed her to a point. That is, nothing was clearly visible or distinct, yet her shape was discernible as the foam flowed around her in frothing waves.

Looking back at him, she felt her body respond to his ardent, smoky gaze as it did to the hot, swirling water—becoming soft and languid, as if her limbs were too heavy to lift.

"Come on in. The water's fine," she mumbled, trying for an even tone. Her voice came out husky, but not too bad, considering the way she felt.

Although she was no longer frightened by the phantom of the woods, she wished Rafe would come to her and hold her... just for a while... until she felt secure.

He stuck his hands into his pockets and gave her a slow once-over. "No, thanks. I haven't the time or the interest to play at the games you women devise to torture men."

"Your eyes say different," she murmured, knowing she was treading on dangerous ground.

"I didn't say I wouldn't like to have sex with you. If that's what you want, I'm willing."

She studied him from half-closed eyes. "You've changed," she finally decided, regret in her voice. "The callous, indifferent male doesn't fit your image."

"How would you know?" he challenged. "You knew me for six weeks almost three years ago, hardly enough time to discover my favorite color, much less my character traits."

"Green," she said. "You like the color of living things around you."

He gave a snort of derision.

She let her gaze wander over him, noting how fit and handsome he looked. A man in his prime, a fit mate for any woman.

No, not any woman. *Her.* Rafe belonged to her!

The thought caught in her throat. She'd never been the jealous, possessive type. Maybe she had traits of her own she didn't know about.

Perhaps that was why she was really here. She wanted to find out about herself and her needs as well as his. "As to character traits, you're stubborn, intelligent, stubborn, candid, stubborn, honest, stubborn—"

"I think I get the picture," he retorted. "You'd better get out of there. It can drop your blood pressure pretty low."

She thought it probably needed lowering. With him around, she was definitely in a high state of tension.

"I don't think I can move," she said, smiling languidly, knowing she was being provocative...and not caring.

She'd always tried to be honest about her feelings, especially with herself. She wanted to flirt with him, to laugh and provoke and play like lovers do when they're falling in love. She wanted those first moments all over again.

He frowned, then walked out.

Closing her eyes, she let the tension drain out of her. Once, she would have sworn he was the most steadfast of men. Now she'd have to say he was one of the most unpredictable creatures she'd ever met.

It was hard to believe Rafe felt he was in any way at fault for an act of terrorism by a mercenary. He knew there was no predicting things like that. Everyone in the diplomatic corps was warned of the personal danger involved in foreign service.

Somehow she had to help him past that. She knew he wanted her. Perhaps she could use that as a lever into his heart and make him see he wasn't responsible for other people's actions or their decisions.

However, their personal problems would have to come second, after the danger was past. But, some part of her whispered, if she were sleeping in his bed, they would both be much safer, wouldn't they?

Before she could summon the energy to chide herself for that insidious thought, he returned.

She got a glimpse of snug blue trunks against well-muscled thighs before he slipped into the water. Lots of hair on his legs, she noticed, and smiled at him.

A pang of alarm went through her as he raked her over with a slow perusal. "Never done this with a man before?" he asked in a drawl, his eyes filled with reckless daring.

"No," she said, answering him seriously. She moved over, feeling uneasy with the hard desire she saw in his eyes. She wanted the passion, but she wanted more. She lifted a hand to his cheek. "What happened to the tenderness?"

He caught her hand and turned her palm to his lips. "I don't know what you're talking about."

"That day at the desert spring. You were passionate, but tender, too."

His face hardened. "Forget then. This is now. You invited me to join you. You've been issuing invitations with your eyes since you arrived. Are you changing your mind?"

"I don't know," she said candidly. "When I respond to you, it seems to make you furious. You think your desire for me is a weakness and you hate me for it."

He leaned toward her. "No," he said in a husky voice. "I don't hate you." He dipped his head and kissed her.

She felt his tongue stroke her lips. He touched one corner of her mouth, sending tingles cascading down her neck and into her breasts. In spite of the heat of the spa, her nipples contracted into hard, jutting points.

Her mouth trembled. He paused, lifting the pressure of his kiss slightly, then his tongue flicked over her lips again, this time pressing between, demanding entry.

Breathing became difficult, but if she opened her mouth to draw air, he would take advantage of the moment. To her relieved surprise, he lifted his head.

His eyes were like dark pools of passion as he gazed at her. No smile lit his face to lend tenderness to his seduction. She saw only the hunger and the hard edge of suppressed anger.

Doubts tore at her. She wanted him to come to her in joy and mutual sharing, not in the passion of the moment.

"Rafe—"

He took her by ambush, his mouth slamming gently down on hers. His tongue joined the attack, sweeping inside to taste and savor and nourish the rising need in her.

With a low moan, she let him take the intimate kiss. Time fell away, and it was like their first kiss—all eager searching and exploring, wanting to know the other fully. She felt his hands on her face, cupping her head to hold her in place.

Lifting a hand from the foamy water, she held on to his wrist and pushed herself higher in the whirlpool, meeting kiss with kiss, answering each thrust of his tongue.

He groaned her name as if the passion were a hot knife searing him with desire. Slowly, he moved his hand over her.

She held her breath, then felt the warm trail of his fingers on her neck, her collarbone, her shoulder, her arm. Midway along her arm, his hand in the warm, whirling water, he retraced the path to her throat, then moved down to the taut skin of her breast.

A sigh escaped her when he closed his hand over her, squeezing in a kneading pattern. She was as pliable and light as rising bread dough. When he moved away from her, she felt bereft.

Opening her eyes—it took such an effort—she watched him for a second before she realized he was standing, then peeling out of his trunks.

Her heart went wild. She gave a choked gasp. He was magnificent . . . simply magnificent, his body lean and hard-looking with ripples of muscle like a well-cared-for machine.

He glanced at her. "It's too late to protest," he told her, his eyes dark with passion, their expression wary.

"I'm not protesting."

Still holding her gaze, he stepped into the hot tub. The water rose past his thighs, then his hips and waist. He sat beside her and pulled her across his lap, cradling her head against his shoulder. The bubbles eddied around them like soft, wet kisses.

She stroked his lean cheek, then slipped her hand behind his head when his mouth met hers again. The rush of emotion that flowed through her was almost painful in its intensity.

No one but Rafe had ever made her feel like this—as if the world were beginning and ending all at once.

The moist suction of his lips against hers drove sensations like lightning bolts deep into her body. She was consumed by needs that had never been fulfilled, needs that only he brought to life. She tightened her arms around him, wanting more and more and more.

He responded with the sultry probe of his tongue against hers. She clung to him helplessly, shamelessly.

His hand smoothed down her back, followed the groove of her spine and slipped between her buttocks to explore intimately.

"You have the smoothest skin," he whispered, breaking the kiss to wander over her face, leaving little, moist, burning places as he trailed his tongue over her, tasting and nibbling with his lips.

She heard the sounds of their breathing over the rippling of the water. The tiny moans that tore out of her throat as he caressed the most sensitive parts of her and the pounding of their hearts seemed as one grand melody, the harmonies fusing and rushing together in a wonderful song of need and desire... and love.

He teased her nipples with his long, lean fingers before lifting her, until he could lick and bite at them in playful battle.

"I love your touch," she said in a near sob, pressing frantic kisses on his forehead and hair. "I'd never dreamed of passion like this—so harsh and hungry and sweet...oh, so sweet."

"Yes, sweet," he echoed, letting her slide down so that she straddled his lap.

His hands at her hips pulled her tight against the hard length of his arousal. Slowly he guided her up and down in an erotic movement that had them both gasping.

"Be still," he ordered hoarsely. He wrapped his arms around her and pressed his face into her shoulder.

She waited, wild for release, yet wanting the closeness, the touching, to go on forever. The tension doubled.

He raised his head on a deeply drawn breath. His gaze roamed her face. She knew she was flushed, her hair a mass of tangles and wet, rat-tail ends. He seemed to find her beautiful.

"Your eyes looked the same that day in the desert. I never think of you, but I think of the heat and light, the shadows of the palms dancing over us," she whispered dreamily.

At the mention of the desert, his eyes went darker. She regretted her ill-chosen words.

She felt the withdrawal before he even started, so she wasn't surprised when he lifted her from him and climbed out of the spa.

He grabbed a towel from the stack and wrapped it around his waist. "You're just a woman," he said. "I can control this."

"For how long?" she questioned, lost without his arms to hold her. Even in the swirling water, she felt the icy depths of his regard.

"Until you leave."

She thought of several replies and opted for a question. "Why do you hate me? What have I done?" she cried softly, baffled. She sprang from the tub and put a detaining hand on his arm.

He looked at her flushed body, then into her eyes. "I hate what you do to me, what you make me feel," he said in a voice that chilled her soul. "You make me forget honor, loyalty, everything."

He walked out, leaving her there, stunned by his words. The door closed behind him. The soft click was like the slam of a gate, barring her from all hope of a future with him.

"I want to go," Genny told the agent. She'd stood at the bottom of the steps and intercepted him as he came by with the snowblower. The noise of its engine grated on her nerves.

He cut the motor to idle and studied her for a second. She waited, determined to hold her silence.

"You can't," he finally said. "Things are going well. Rafe is alert. He keeps a sharp eye out for situations—"

"Like assassins behind trees?" she scoffed angrily. "I've read the articles. There's really no protection. Why don't you tell him the truth and make him leave until you find the guy?"

"In spite of what most people think of the federal government, we can't order people around arbitrarily. Rafe is a private citizen. We can't force him to go to a safe house." Deveraux's face became guarded. "This is the best chance we have of catching our man. I don't want you telling Barrett anything that would cause him to take any unnecessary risk. For you, he'll be careful. For himself…" He shrugged.

"He'd act foolhardy," she concluded. "I'm not sure he'll be all that careful because of me. Things are difficult between us," she told him, laying it on the line.

"You knew they would be when you came here."

"I think I could hate you," she said, angered at his attitude.

He flashed her one of his rare, stunning smiles that belied his seemingly indifferent manner. "Get in line."

She smiled ruefully. "It's probably too long for me to wait my turn."

That drew a laugh from him. "If you still have your sense of humor, you're doing okay. Cat-and-mouse games are nerve-racking, especially if you're a new player. And if your emotions are involved, as I think yours are…"

She didn't respond to the quizzical lift of his brows. The agent had been against her coming there. Rafe's father had insisted. Sighing, she admitted she didn't understand the father any better than she did the son. If Mr. Barrett thought she could reach inside Rafe and unlock his soul from whatever bound it, he was mistaken. Rafe kept his own counsel.

"Hang in there for a while longer," Deveraux advised. "We need Barrett to be on guard. We've lost track of our man."

Her head jerked up. "What do you mean, you've lost track of him? How? Where?"

"New York. We were closing in, then he disappeared without a trace. He's a master at disguise. The local police have two detectives staked out at the lodge. We'll be ready when our man shows himself."

"'Our man,'" she repeated. A shiver ran over her. "Mad Dog is a better name for him. We don't know when or how he'll strike."

"But we know where, and we know he's out there. He doesn't know about us."

She stared off toward the lodge, out of sight because of the woods between. "Okay. I'll stay. But I have to have something to do during the day, else I'll go mad."

"Complain to Barrett. Maybe he'll give you a job." The agent flicked the machine back to full speed and started working on the piles of snow again.

"I'll do that," she yelled over the noise. "Right now."

He nodded, grinned and moved off. She noted the green handkerchief hanging out of his jacket pocket before she started down the path. Three days of being cooped up was more than she could stand. She stomped off.

The office door was open when she stormed in. Rafe and a redheaded woman were bent over the desk, their heads almost touching as they looked at photographs.

A shaft of hot jealousy streaked through Genny. She wanted to order the woman away from Rafe. Folding her arms over her chest, she grasped at control. She had to get over the crazy notion that he belonged to *her*.

"May I help you?" the woman asked.

"I'm here to see Rafe."

He favored her with one of the bleak scowls he'd worn around her for the past three days, since the episode in the hot tub.

The woman glanced at Rafe with a question in her eyes.

Genny glared at her. Who did the redhead think she was, his personal bodyguard?

"It's Genny," he said to the woman.

She beamed at Genny in obvious delight. "Hi, Genny. I'm Val. I spoke to you Saturday when you called, if you remember."

Genny felt her face heat up. Nothing like making a total fool of oneself. She gave Rafe a killing glance, then summoned up a bright smile for his assistant manager. "Hello, Val. Yes, of course, I remember. I'm glad to meet you."

Rafe broke into the getting-acquainted chat. "What are you doing out?"

"Looking for something to do." She faced him, locking her gaze with his, refusing to be intimidated by his scowl...or his hatred. "I want a job. Do you have an opening?"

"I'll, uh, check with you later on the photo layout," Val said as she quickly departed. She closed the door behind her.

"Have you spoken to Deveraux?" he snapped.

"Yes. He knows I'm here."

A silent tug-of-war took place between them. She held her ground, although her knees got a bit shaky. Finally he swung around, sat down in his chair and motioned her to take a seat.

She pulled the chair to the side of his desk and sat down.

"What can you do?" he asked coolly.

"I can translate. Do you have any foreign correspondence?"

"No."

"My typing is a little rusty," she ventured after an icy silence. "But I can brush up—"

"Val takes care of all that."

"Maybe I can clerk in one of the stores. Who does the hiring for those?"

"Val if we own the place, the manager if it's a chain."

"Waitress?"

"No."

"What other jobs do you have?"

His smile was triumphant. "Ski patrol."

Despair settled on her shoulders. "I know you don't want me here," she said after a lengthy pause. "I'd leave if I could, but Deveraux said—"

"So you've already asked," Rafe interjected. "Undercover work isn't quite as exciting as James Bond makes it out to be, is it?"

"No."

Rafe picked up a pen and clicked the ballpoint in and out. The noise grated on her nerves. He threw the pen down. It rolled across the desk and fell to the floor. With an oath, he picked it up and tossed it in a pencil mug.

"Do you have a job for me?" she persisted.

"I have to be out of the office the rest of the day. Do you think you can answer the telephone and take messages?" His glance held the certainty that she would refuse.

She lifted her chin. "Yes, I can do that. Where will you be? In case I need to reach you," she added at his none-of-your-business glance.

"I wear a beeper. Val knows my number."

"Do I work in here, or is there an office I can use?"

"Here. This is my private line. You take care of it. Val handles the resort stuff." He stood. "I'll tell her to put you on the payroll."

"I don't want your money!"

One dark eyebrow lifted imperiously. "You should always get paid for your work," he advised, and walked out.

"I am," she called out, but he was gone. She'd have to ask Deveraux about the ethics of accepting a salary since she was on paid leave. She realized the agent was working for the resort, so presumably he got double pay.

Giving up on ethics, she surveyed the room, looking for clues to the man who'd turned his back on a promising foreign service career. It was well known he'd been on the "fast track" and would make ambassador before he was forty.

She stood at the window and observed the bustling resort. Rafe was so capable at whatever he did. He accomplished whatever he set out to do. She settled in his chair with her feet drawn under her after kicking off her shoes.

Her black wool slacks and gold sweater were more than formal enough for a resort office. Val had worn a pair of faded cords—very snug-fitting, faded cords—and a sweater with a vest over it. She had a very shapely bosom.

Genny glanced down. She wasn't large, but Rafe didn't seem to mind. He seemed to find her body irresistible . . . well, almost. Always, before he came to her completely, his conscience stopped him. She had to help him get over his guilt about the past.

She hugged her arms across her chest. She'd hardly slept since Sunday night. Each time she drifted into sleep, she dreamed of the way he'd touched her—as if he couldn't get enough. Then she'd see the terrible, raw pain . . . hunger . . . loathing in his eyes when he'd told her he hated what she did to him.

The hurt of that rejection lingered in her subconscious like a festering splinter, and the fact that he blamed her for the desire that bloomed the moment they were together.

"It's not my fault," she said to the room that was decorated in forest green and shades of mauve. "It happens to me, too."

She sighed and laid her head back against the wing chair. For three hours, she waited for a call. None came. Val answered the resort line. Rafe got no calls on his private line.

At three, she wandered into Val's office. The assistant manager glanced up with a smile and a question in her expression.

"Do you have any filing you'd like done?" Genny inquired with a glum smile.

"Um, yes, as a matter of fact, I do." She pointed to a basket on the table behind her. It was labeled File.

Val showed her how the correspondence file was sorted. Genny set to work. By five, she had the office shipshape.

"What time will Rafe be back?" she asked when Val indicated she was ready to lock up.

Val gave her a sympathetic smile. "I don't know. I have no idea where he is."

Alarm shot through Genny. "He is here at the resort, isn't he?" She'd thought he was out checking on the ski operations.

"I saw him leave in his car. I assumed he was going to Medford to run some errands. That's where we bank."

"Can you page him?"

"Yes. Is there something wrong?"

Genny realized she was overreacting again. She forced herself to relax. Deveraux and the other two men had everything under control. They'd know whether it was safe to leave.

"No, I was just wondering."

Val stood and pushed her hands through her hair. It fell around her shoulders in attractive disarray.

"Are you a natural redhead?" Genny asked.

The other woman laughed and shook her head. "Brown. Dull as dishwater. I use henna to brighten it."

"It looks nice."

"Thanks." Val studied Genny thoughtfully. "You know, we decided not to have a social director this year, but I think we need one. Would you like to try it?"

"A social director?" Genny looked doubtful. "I don't even know what one does."

"Plans things," Val promptly supplied. "Puts together some hikes and picnics in the woods—"

"In this weather?"

Val waved the problem of eight feet of snow aside. "People love the idea of an adventure. They're into this macho-health-nut stuff these days. You know—open air, exercise, fruit and whole wheat bread, that sort of thing."

"Well..."

"It'll be fun," Val assured her. "I'll help you." A sardonic smile touched her wide mouth. "The maintenance supervisor will, too. He flirts with everyone in sight. Women love him."

Genny studied Val while the woman locked up, then went outside with her. They said farewell at the path. Val was in love with the supervisor, Genny decided. He obviously hadn't a clue.

Men.

Rafe tried the door and found it locked. He used his key to let himself into the town house. It was after midnight. He was dog-tired after dealing with bankers and lawyers all day, then going to dinner with them at his banker's insistence.

He glanced back down the path, aware that he'd been trailed all day by a local cop in plain clothes. He'd resisted the urge to walk up to the man and tell him to get the hell back here and watch out for Genny.

With her staying at his place, he wasn't such a fool as to think he wasn't in danger, too. He didn't think she'd grasped that fact, yet. And he didn't intend for her to.

After tossing off his parka and laying his briefcase on the table, he headed up the stairs. He didn't think about his motive for doing so. He just had a need to check on her, to see that she was all right.

She was.

Her face was barely visible above the covers, which were tucked in around her shoulders and pulled tight to her chin.

He couldn't help but smile. She looked so innocent in her sleep, with none of her guileful ways.

But his own thoughts weren't so innocent, he acknowledged. He wanted to strip out of his clothes and slip into that warm cocoon with her. He wanted to kiss her awake and see her bloom with the passion he could give her. He wanted to lose himself in her, to luxuriate in her warmth and sweetness.

Yes, and there lay the problem.

When he touched her, he forgot everything but that one fact—the feel of her...the heat. Touching Genny was like touching the sun. Her warmth . . . the life-giving warmth.

Inside, he felt the cold shift and tremble like an iceberg giving way from a glacier. He'd been cold for so long, he'd forgotten there was warmth and laughter in the world.

He clenched his fists. Life was better this way. He'd rather have the cold. It numbed the pain.

For a second he saw the car that Tom and the diplomat had been riding in. It had been a burned-out wreck, nothing but scrap metal left. The experts had had to use dental records to confirm the occupants of the diplomatic vehicle.

He should have been one of those occupants.

The cold shifted again. He stared into the darkness that was his soul. When Genny had appeared, she'd brought light and warmth.

Maybe he wasn't to blame for Tom's death. Maybe she was right. They had all made choices. But now, here, if he became lost in her magic and she died, who would give him absolution?

"Who?" he murmured to her. "No one. Not ever."

He had to keep his head clear so he could protect her. For her to die...

His heart swelled with anger and a pain so profound it ripped into his soul. He put a hand to his aching chest and tried not to think of death and the horrors that accompanied it.

Genny was too inexperienced to visualize death, especially to herself. He wasn't. He'd seen the innocent suffer to the point that death was a relief.

"I'll keep you safe," he promised in a low, almost voiceless growl. "Nothing, not even you and your compelling passion, will stop me."

Chapter Six

Genny was ready when Rafe left for the office the next morning. Ignoring his forbidding expression, she chatted to him as if she hadn't a care in the world.

Little Miss Sunshine. Ha!

"I'm not sure what a social director does, but Val said she and Bill Somebody—the maintenance supervisor?—would help me."

"Like hell," Rafe muttered.

"I beg your pardon?" She cast him a sunny smile. When he didn't respond, she continued. "It sounds like fun. And it's a real job, not like answering a telephone that never rings."

He gave a snort. "I don't have much of a private life."

"You don't have any. Why not?"

"You adding Lonely Hearts Club to your agenda?" The ice shards in his voice nearly pierced her determined cheer.

"Are you a candidate?" She lowered her head and swept her lashes up when he glared at her—a flirtatious move if there ever was one.

He caught her wrist and swung her around so that she landed with a soft plop against his hard chest. She gazed into his face and tried to read his intent. Only that hard-edged passion was clearly visible. He kept other emotions locked out of sight.

"Don't come on to me unless you're willing to pay the full price," he snarled.

She swallowed nervously. He looked like a man nearing the end of his rope. When he got there, he might tie a noose in it and hoist her over the nearest tree limb.

"What price?" It was hard to speak, she was so breathless.

He glared at her for another second. The bleakness returned to his eyes, and he pushed her away. With a quick glance all around, he started down the path.

"Come on," he ordered.

His face became even more closed. Genny felt the icy hand of despair clutch at her. She sighed. She'd better keep her mind on her new job and forget about him for the time being.

Val was at her desk when they went inside. She took in Rafe's frown and Genny's determined smile. "Um, he didn't like the idea of social director, huh?"

"Uh, no," Genny confirmed.

"It's okay," he said.

Both women stared at him.

"It's a good idea," he continued. "You'll be among people. You'll be busy. That'll give you less chance of getting into trouble. I should have thought of it."

Genny realized he was taking sole responsibility for her, not only her safety, but her general well-being. It gave her a funny feeling inside. He wasn't quite as unapproachable as he pretended.

"Well," Val said, a surprised smile lighting her face.

Rafe spoke directly to Genny. "You'll stay inside the lodge at all times, unless I'm with you. Is that clear?"

"Aye, aye, sir."

He narrowed his eyes at her, but he didn't reprimand her smart answer. "Can she work in here?" he asked Val.

"Sure. I'll clean off the table by the window."

He went over and checked the view from all angles.

"Excuse me, boss," Val said, "but do I detect something clandestine going on here?"

"Keep it under your hat," Rafe advised without giving a direct yea or nay.

"I would," she replied, "if I knew what it was."

Rafe sighed in obvious exasperation. "It's nothing you need be concerned about." He paused. "But if you hear shots, hit the floor."

Val's eyes widened. "That's nothing to worry about?"

He frowned at his assistant. "Just stay out of it. You're not in any danger if you stay out of the way."

Val's gaze swung to Genny. "It's Genny, isn't it? That's why you're so protective of her."

"Enough said," Rafe ordered. "Everything is under control. No one is in danger... except maybe an assistant manager and a social director if they don't get to work."

Val cast Genny a sympathetic, albeit worried, glance. Genny summoned up courage she didn't feel and smiled reassuringly at Val.

This operation was getting more complicated as additional people were sucked in. She considered telling Val what was going on, in case something happened. She'd ask Deveraux.

"Well," she said brightly. "To work. What's first on my agenda? Or do I have one?"

Rafe went into his office while Val explained. "Tonight's Friday. The social director used to serve hot snacks and circulate among the guests in the lounge here."

When Rafe's door closed, Genny asked Val in a lowered tone, "What happened to the former social director?"

"She made the mistake of falling in love with the boss."

"And?"

"She was fired when she said some catty things to a guest who was making a play for him. She, uh, thought he was her property."

"I see." Genny wondered if the social director and Rafe had been having an affair. Hot licks of jealousy flamed through her. "If anybody comes on to him while I'm around, I'll pull her hair out. And maybe his, too, for good measure."

Val clamped a hand over her mouth and spluttered with laughter. "I see things are going to be lively here with you around."

"Right. Who do I consult about the hot snacks?"

Rafe leaned against the bar and hooked his toes under the rung of the stool. Genny was parading around the lounge area in a red skirt that covered her to midthigh. She wore black boots, a wide black belt and a white sweater. Every time he looked at her, he got hard. *Damn.*

She'd found a guy who could play the piano and was conducting a sing-along. Right now the crowd was singing "Row, Row, Row Your Boat" in rounds and having a rousing good time at it. He couldn't believe she'd gotten grown people to do this.

Genny would make a wonderful wife for a diplomat, he realized. She was friendly and natural with people. He looked away as a hard lump the size of a boulder settled in his chest.

He surveyed the noisy crowd. Usually the older guests came here and the younger ones went to the Moosehead. He wasn't about to let Genny traipse down there. Too isolated.

Deveraux thought this job was a good idea. He hoped it would draw the mercenary to the lodge so they could spot him. Unless he'd changed his appearance again.

Rafe laughed mockingly, silently. Hell, he didn't even know what the guy looked like. He only had a gut feeling and a quick eye for anything out of the ordinary to offer for protection. The agent seemed to think that was enough.

"Stay alert," was his constant advice.

As if Rafe could be anything else around Genny. She kept him in a state of excitement....

He stopped his musing and scrutinized one guest who sat in the corner, not participating in the singing, but watching Genny with an intensity that seemed off-key.

Rafe carefully let his gaze flicker past the man and observed him from the periphery of his vision. He felt a tightening inside, the coiled-spring tension of danger.

The man was big and blond, a Nordic type, which didn't fit the description of the man Deveraux had described. Still, it paid to check these things out. Just then, a woman came over and sat at the table. The man turned to her with a smile, the tense look gone from his expression. Maybe he'd been thinking of something besides Genny...some business or personal problem.

Rafe could relate to that. His gaze went to Genny as she ended the singing, then thanked everybody for participating. Her face was flushed. Her eyes sparkled.

God, she was beautiful. He'd thought so the first time he'd seen her. He still did.

She was like the sun, the giver of life....

"Ready?"

He had to clear his throat before he could speak. "Yeah."

"How do you think it went?" She peered over her shoulder at him when he held her coat for her, her eyes anxious now.

"Fine."

"Good. I was nervous at first, but I thought things went okay, too, especially when Jim agreed to play for us. That was nice, wasn't it?"

"Yeah. Let's go."

She stopped her chatter at his brusque tone and fell into step beside him. They left the lodge and headed up the lighted path.

The moon was out tonight. It cast a luminous glow on the landscape, enhancing the beauty of the Christmas card scene. He heard Genny give a tired sigh.

He'd hurt her feelings. She didn't make a big deal over it like most women, but he knew he had.

He cleared his throat. "I didn't realize you had such a good voice. I was surprised when you and Jim harmonized on that song. It sounded as if you'd been practicing for months."

She cast him a quick glance, then looked back at the path. "He was the one who harmonized. I just carried the melody."

"Still, it's something to be able to do that."

Her smile flashed white in the moonlight, then was gone. "I've often thought you must have a good singing voice."

"I don't sing," he stated.

"Why not?"

He looked at the way the light cast shadows under her cheekbones. Her lips looked soft and vulnerable. "I don't know."

She laughed. "Men," she said, as if that explained his lack of singing.

Rafe noted the way her hair clung to the collar of her coat. Static electricity. He felt like he was carrying a lethal charge. If he touched her, he'd vaporize them both.

He looked around. Another couple followed them on the path. The Nordic twosome. Had he seen them at the town houses?

Genny glanced around. "The honeymooners," she whispered, leaning close to him. "Val thinks they had a quarrel. They weren't speaking at breakfast. Looks like all is well."

Rafe took her hand. "Quiet," he said. He pulled her off the trail and behind a tree.

He was aware of her questioning gaze, but she stayed silent until the other couple had passed and was well in front of them.

"What was that all about?" she asked.

"This," he said.

Without letting himself think, he pulled her into his arms. He caught a glimpse of her surprise, then the bright glow of pleasure on her face when he kissed her. The kiss went on a long time. When she shivered, he released her, his breath coming hard.

They walked on up the path.

At the porch, he looked back before opening the door. A dark shape stepped out of the trees. The man took a handkerchief that dangled out of his pocket and blew his nose. He put the hankie away and walked off. He was soon out of sight.

Rafe felt the anger return. Some guard he was. Whenever he was alone with Genny, all he wanted was to make love to her. If he forgot himself at the wrong moment, Genny would end up dead. How could he live with that for the rest of his life?

Answer: he couldn't.

Genny found she was too restless to sleep after the tension of the evening. She'd been afraid she would be a failure as a hostess, but she'd pulled it off okay. That, plus Rafe's kiss there on the path, added up to insomnia.

Slipping into her robe and moccasins, she padded downstairs and into the den. She was startled to see a fire in there.

"Leave the light out," Rafe said in a husky tone. He was lying on one of the sofas, his hands behind his head while he watched the firelight play over the logs. His sock-clad feet hung over the end.

She settled in the corner of the other sofa and drew her feet up under her. She watched the fire for a while, then gazed out at the moonlight on the snow.

"It's so beautiful here," she murmured dreamily. "It's no wonder you decided to stay."

"My father wants me back in the service."

"I know." She saw tension enter the set of his shoulders. "Will you ever go back?"

"No."

"Because of what happened to Tom?"

He was silent so long, she thought he wasn't going to answer. "No." His voice was strained. It reminded her of the dry crackle of crushed leaves in the fall. "You were right. We each make our choices. I've made mine. I won't go back."

She nodded in understanding.

"Did my father ask you to talk to me about returning?"

"Yes, but I refused." She caught the flicker of surprise from him at her statement. "The decision was yours."

Rafe laughed, a dark, brooding sound, as dangerous as the night and the tension that escalated by the minute between them.

"He sent the one person guaranteed to bring me to heel." He was obviously bitter about it.

"Me?" she asked, her breath strangling in her throat.

"Of course, you."

She didn't know what to say. If that was a confession of love, it was different from any she'd ever heard. It sounded more like an accusation...of someone he didn't like very much.

"You realize an involvement is out of the question," he said, as if expounding on a scientific discovery.

"Why?"

"Because I said." He stood, preparing to leave.

"Don't I have any say in our lives?"

"No." Instead of leaving, he added another log to the fire, closed the glass doors and adjusted the airflow vents. He turned and looked at her, his face cast into shadow. "People could die if we were involved. That's reason enough."

She had a sudden vision of Rafe lying in the snow—the cold purity of white all around, while from his chest poured his life's blood...red...red all over him. She shook her head.

"I couldn't bear for you to be hurt," she whispered through an aching throat.

"It's too late to think of that. No house can be completely safe. That's why passion is out. It causes a man to make mistakes and forget his goal. I won't take that chance with you."

Understanding dawned on her. "You do want me."

His laughter mocked her. "Like hell. Don't play your flirting games with me, Genny. I haven't the time."

"I understand."

He was protecting them from the carelessness brought on by passion. She shivered. One inattentive moment and their lives could be snuffed out like a candle. The danger felt closer, although Deveraux had told her only that afternoon that he was sure all was clear for now.

"I'm not afraid to take chances," she said.

He looked momentarily irritated, but he didn't pursue the matter. She looked at him hungrily, wanting the closeness of his arms around her. Whatever came, she was prepared to meet it.

"I don't know what to do with you," Rafe said. He set his coffee cup down and flicked her a hard glance.

She glared back. "You know, I've been on my own for a long time now. I don't like being treated like a package that has to be shuffled around from place to place."

He assessed her mood. "Touchy this morning, aren't you? Didn't you sleep well?" he inquired with mock concern.

"Didn't you?" she countered.

"No."

She sighed. This verbal jousting was silly. Sometimes she forgot about the danger and that she was supposed to encourage him to watch out for her. Their personal problems seemed much more real and pressing than some weirdo lurking in the woods.

The tension between her and her reluctant host was so strong, it was almost visible.

"Why can't I work in Val's office like I did yesterday?" she asked on a quieter note.

"Val won't be in this weekend. She's visiting her sister so they can do their Christmas shopping."

Christmas. Genny looked at the wall calendar. December had sneaked up on her. She'd be expected at her parents' home for the holidays, along with her two sisters and their husbands and kids. "Do you go to the embassy during Christmas?"

"No."

She thought of him alone here in his cold aerie—no family to provide warmth and cheer, none of the noise and confusion that goes with Christmas morning and gift opening, no tree but the impersonal one at the lodge. "You stay here?"

"Don't look so aghast. It isn't the worst thing that can happen," he snapped.

She looked down at the steam rising off the coffee cup and tried not to think of his being alone. He'd never admit he was lonely.

He sighed loudly. "My sister and her family have a ranch a couple of hours from here. My parents and I are invited to spend the holidays there."

Genny smiled happily. "That's good. No one should be alone during Christmas."

"You'd better watch that soft heart," he suggested coolly. "It'll get you into trouble one day."

She wrinkled her nose at him. "I can be tough," she warned. "Now, let's see. I need to check the notice about the hike and picnic scheduled for tomorrow to see if anyone signed up. Then I need to order the lunches."

Rafe stood. "Get your coat."

"Am I going to the office?" she asked.

"You'll spend the day with me." He left the kitchen and went into his room.

Genny was relieved. He didn't look very happy about having her tag along, but he obviously felt he had to keep an eye on her. Good. He'd be careful about where they went. With her along, he'd make sure they stayed close to other people.

She pulled on her parka and her new suede shoes with the thick soles that were great for navigating icy walkways. After checking the thermometer on the porch—thirty degrees, a heat wave!—she decided to wear her fuzzy mittens rather than her heavy ski gloves.

With her tote clipped around her waist and her toboggan hat on, she was ready. Rafe returned from his room. He wore the sweater she liked, plus a Windbreaker and the down vest.

"Ready?"

She nodded, aware of his eyes on her, checking her over. With his hazel eyes of brown, green and gold and hers of mostly green, their children would surely have hazel-green eyes. She put the intriguing fantasy out of her mind and followed Rafe out and down the path.

"Your sister had a little boy, if I remember correctly. Does she have other children now?"

"A girl."

"That's what I want—a boy and a girl," Genny murmured. "A ranch sounds like a wonderful place to raise kids."

"The great American myth," Rafe scoffed. "Everyone wants to be a cowboy."

"I know." She refused to be drawn into an argument. "But it has a certain enduring charm. My grandparents had a farm when I was little. They sold it and retired to a house in town when I was eight. I was terribly disappointed. I had planned to live with them when I grew up."

He gave a grunt, which could have been sympathy or, most likely, indifference.

"What were your dreams when you were a child?"

"I didn't have any."

"Everyone has dreams," she said, scolding him softly.

"Whatever they were, I got over them fast enough." He laughed briefly, mocking whatever vision her question had conjured up.

"What are your dreams now?" she challenged.

He didn't answer.

"It isn't wrong to have them," she told him, worried about his lack of response.

His father had been right. Rafe had closed off a vital part of himself from life. He would drift into lonely old age without ever knowing the joy of his own family.

She remembered the tenderness she'd seen in him, his love of children when they'd visited the goatherd's family. There were so many good qualities in him. She couldn't let them go to waste.

He ignored her and walked faster. When they reached the lodge, he waited while she checked the notice board. She had fifteen people who'd signed up for the hike.

"Look!" she exclaimed, waving the list at Rafe. "I need to tell the cook how many lunches we'll need."

"I'll be in the office," Rafe said.

She dashed up the stairs to the lodge kitchen. She realized Rafe had let her go by herself. He was obviously giving her a little slack. So she wouldn't do something foolish, as he no doubt thought she would.

After talking to the chef in charge of the huge kitchen, she headed back down the stairs. She wondered if Rafe would come on the hike, and felt a tiny thrill at the thought. Perhaps she could lure him into having some fun.

"Well, hello," a masculine voice interrupted her musing as she opened the door to Val's office. "You a new worker?"

The man was tall and lean, with the tanned, rugged features of an outdoorsman. He looked a bit older than Rafe and had a good measure of gray in his dark hair. His eyes crinkled attractively at the corners when he smiled.

"Well, sort of," she admitted. "Val talked me into taking on the social director position. I'm not sure whether she did me a favor or not."

He had a very deep, very attractive laugh. "You're the one I want, then. I'm supposed to help you with a hike tomorrow." There was a question in the statement.

"You're Bill," she concluded.

"Right."

She could see why Val was attracted to him. He had a ready smile and a take-charge manner that were very appealing. "I'm Genny McBride. How's the path to the lookout at Granite Ridge? Will it be too hard for fifteen dudes who are probably out of shape to attempt it?"

"Nah," he drawled. "I'll have one of the men run over it on a snowmobile to pack it down. That'll make it an easy walk."

"Oh, thanks. That would be perfect."

"Do I detect a bit of Texas in that accent?" he asked.

Genny shook her head. "Oklahoma, maybe. I used to visit my grandparents there most summers. I'm from Wichita."

"Where in Oklahoma?"

"Near Pawhuska."

He stuck out his hand. "Heck, we were neighbors. I'm from Bartlesville myself."

She laughed and shook his hand. "Pleased to meet you," she said, as she dipped him a little curtsy the way her grandmother had taught her as a child.

The door between the offices opened. Rafe gave them a scowl. "Bill, could I see you for a minute?"

"Sure." Bill winked at Genny, then ambled into Rafe's office. The door closed behind the two men.

She resisted an impulse to press her ear to the panel to see if she could hear what Rafe had to say. He hadn't looked too pleased to see her and Bill shaking hands. She'd never been one to use male sexual jealousy for her own purposes, but sometimes the ends justified the means.

A clamor from her conscience made her put that idea aside. He already disliked the influence of passion between them. She couldn't use it against him, not even to help him.

After Bill left, coming through Val's office to tell Genny he'd see her at ten-thirty tomorrow for the hike, Rafe came in.

"We'll go on a tour of the place, then I'm going to the top to check out the new run. The ski patrol wants to add another black diamond to its classification. We'll have lunch when I get back. You want to wait in the restaurant?"

"Yes, that'll be fine."

She spent the rest of the morning trailing at his heels while he checked out all the operations of the resort. The crowd was heavy that weekend, she noted. At eleven, he left her at the table he usually used at the restaurant and headed for the slopes.

In a minute, she saw him drop his skis onto the snow and step into them. He skied down to one of the chair lifts. She kept her eyes on him while he rode to the very top of the mountain.

Rogue's Leap was the steepest run on the mountain. She had a perfect view of it from the window. The skiers at the top were few. They looked like moving dots against the snow until they got to the bottom third of the slope. She couldn't tell which one was Rafe after he started down.

She ordered a cup of tea while she waited. She saw Gabriel Deveraux standing near a chair lift, his gaze on the steep run. Her heart clenched in fear. He turned as if he sensed her worry and waved at her.

Reassured, she stirred sugar and cream into her tea when the waitress brought it. She wondered when the agent slept. He always seemed to be around when she and Rafe were out of the town house. She was grateful for his vigilance, but didn't he ever get tired?

A skier swept into view on the last part of the steep course. She recognized Rafe's down vest and the red ski-patrol band he wore around his head to keep his ears warm. Admiration filled her at his smooth form and perfect control. He was an excellent skier.

He came to a stop below the window. When he looked up, she smiled and waved. He hesitated, then waved back. She noticed he didn't say anything to Deveraux, although the man stood no more than ten feet away. Instead Rafe talked to the ski-patrol captain, then carried his skis inside.

When he joined her at the table, she couldn't help the thrill of pride she felt when other women looked at him, then at her, envy on their faces. She had to get over being so possessive of him, she chided. He was not *hers*. He'd let her know that right off.

"Did you have a good run?" she asked.

"It was okay. That slope is definitely a double black diamond," he added, a grin curling the corners of his mouth. "I told the patrol to change the sign. I don't want anybody up there who isn't Olympic material."

He was so handsome, she wanted to lean over and kiss him. Of course she didn't. "That leaves me out," she said.

His gaze flicked over her. "Women don't have to take those kinds of risks to prove their power."

"Do I detect some kind of sexist sneer in that statement?" she demanded, pretending to be offended.

"Does the shoe fit?" he asked sardonically.

"I don't know. Explain what you mean."

"A woman can bend a man to her will by using his passion for her against him."

A hint of a flush heated her face. "Well, sometimes it's the easiest way to get results."

"So you admit you've used your feminine wiles—"

"No," she said sharply. She met his cool gaze. "I've thought about it, but I don't think I ever have, not intentionally."

Instead of disputing her word, he withdrew into his own musing. Finally he murmured, "It would be hell for us men if you ever decided to use that simmering sensuality on purpose."

She nearly choked on her tea. Patting her mouth with a napkin, she stared at him.

"Yeah, the wide-eyed innocent is pretty alluring, too."

"You're the only one who sees me that way," she protested. "Other men don't—"

"Don't they?" he scoffed. "Bill was about ready to lie down and roll over. You only needed to give the command."

"That's not true," she said firmly. The familiar heat caused by his perusal seeped through her.

He had to know she melted whenever he paid her the slightest attention. She'd nearly let him make love to her there in the desert that day...and in the hot tub the other night. He was the one who'd pulled away the second time. That made them even. How would the next round between them go?

"Why did you have to come here?" he asked wearily, catching her off guard.

"I wanted to see if there was something between us, something more than the desire we shared at that first meeting." She paused. "I think there is."

He shook his head. "Danger heightens other emotions. Surely you realize that."

"It can," she admitted. She was silent for a minute. "Why have you shut yourself away up here in the mountains?"

Anger drove the cynical smile from his face. He gave her such a fierce glare, she wondered if she was a fool not to be afraid of him. But she'd seen his tenderness, she reminded herself.

His cool mask slipped into place. "Ah, I think I detect the meddling hands of my family in that question. They finally gave up on my sister once she married her rancher, but apparently they haven't given up on me."

"I don't know about that. It's just that sometimes I get this terrible feeling of loneliness . . . from you."

"I'm not lonely," he stated in a low growl.

Prickles along the back of her neck warned her she was treading too close. Men like Rafe didn't like their emotions explored, not even for their own good.

"I am." She dared to look directly at him, to let him see....

He cursed under his breath. "There are plenty of men around to see that you aren't. Bill, for instance."

"It's strange, isn't it," she murmured in conversational tones, "that not anyone will do, that we want only one?"

The bleakness returned to his eyes, then his gaze turned cold. "I find that hard to believe. You went steady in high school. Surely there were men in college who interested you."

She shook her head. "I didn't meet anyone I really wanted. Until I met you."

He looked skeptical. "But I don't want you...not in any way that's permanent. Don't you understand that?"

She hadn't, but she did now. He'd never felt anything but lust for her. Only she had been foolish enough to think it was love and that it would be there waiting for her after all this time.

The urgent press of tears had her on her feet. She wasn't sure she could control them, and she'd die before she'd cry in front of him. "Excuse me," she said, as she walked out.

Chapter Seven

A hand caught at her arm. "Don't. Let me go," Genny said.

"Not until you calm down," Gabriel Deveraux told her.

The sharp, low-spoken command cut through her misery. She took a deep breath. "I'm all right."

He let go of her arm, looked her over and nodded. "What happened?"

"I took a remark personally when I shouldn't have." She managed a smile. "It's hard on the ego."

"Hmm."

"I'm okay now. Really."

"Hmm."

She saw the worry and speculation in his eyes as he assessed her mood. "For whatever it's worth, you have my word that I'll stick to the job at hand in the future."

He smiled, a brilliant flash of white in his tanned face. "I believe you." He strolled along the trail to the town houses with her. "Stay alert. Don't rush into danger," he advised.

"Right." She smiled wearily.

At the foot of the steps, he bid her goodbye and ambled on as if checking the condition of the pathways. Genny retrieved the key from her tote and opened the door. Before going in, she glanced back down the path to see if Rafe was on it.

In the woods, off to one side of the trail, she saw a man standing among the trees. She froze. The hair prickled on the back of her neck.

She studied the dark shape. No, it wasn't a person, just a shrub in the shadow of a tree. Except the tree was moving with the wind. The shrub wasn't.

Glancing around, she saw the agent was no longer in sight. She didn't know where he'd gone. Her heart lodged in her throat. Think! She had to think what she should do.

Don't rush into danger.

But Rafe was out there. He might be coming along the path at that very moment. He'd be alone. He wouldn't know there was danger in the woods.

She locked the dead bolt again, then headed down the steps. Forcing a calm she was far from feeling, she faced the path without letting herself peer anxiously through the trees. She was in no danger, she reasoned. No one would shoot a person in broad daylight on a path frequently traveled.

Not that the mercenary would think twice about blowing her away, but he'd wait for the cards to be in his favor.

With trembling fingers, she eased open the tote clipped around her waist and felt for the small gun. She was glad the agent had insisted she be trained to use it. If attacked, she wasn't going to go without a protest.

Turning her back to the trees, she pretended to work with the zipper of her jacket. Quickly she transferred the weapon to her pocket, zipped the coat to her neck and turned back down the path.

Ribbons of fear circulated in electric currents along her skin as she marched steadfastly along. She casually scanned the scenery as she walked. Halfway down the upper wooded path, she met another couple coming up. They carried skis over their shoulders and clomped along in their boots, panting with effort.

"Hi. The runs are great," the man said.

"Yes," the woman assured her, "the snow is perfect."

"Super," Genny said.

As if she cared. But skiers always exchanged weather and snow reports, she'd found. She tried to smile naturally, but her lips felt glued to her teeth. She stepped to the side and let them go on up the trail, then resumed her journey.

At the merger of the trails, she took the path to the lodge. Rafe was still at the table.

"I ordered my lunch," he said coolly when she appeared. "I didn't know if you'd be back."

Lunch. Good. That would keep him preoccupied and in a crowd for another hour or so. Maybe Deveraux would show up by then.

"I decided it wasn't wise to skip meals up here. It takes a lot of calories to keep a body warm—"

She stopped her chatter when his gaze darted to her, roaming over her breasts, then to her mouth. There were other ways of keeping a body warm, it seemed to say. A flush seeped into her cheeks, a tingle into her abdomen.

"What happened to your escort?" he asked. "I saw Deveraux join you outside."

"He walked me to the town house and left me there. I decided I'd better head back if I wanted lunch." She picked up the menu and looked over the items, as if food were the only thing on her mind. She sighed wistfully.

After ordering the day's special and a pot of tea, she watched the skiers coming down the various runs off the mountain and kept an eye out for the agent.

She was tempted to tell Rafe what she'd seen and warn him to be careful, but he'd likely think she was seeing things after her scare in the woods the other day. Perhaps she was. Every shape and shadow looked like a villain.

Pressing a hand to her tummy, she wondered how long it took an ulcer to develop.

The waitress brought Rafe's food.

"Have a roll," he invited. "You look hungry."

"Thanks." She accepted one of the delicious home-made rolls the lodge was famous for.

"Butter?"

"No, thanks."

He lifted one eyebrow. "Watching your weight?"

"Not exactly. I've learned to eat most foods without added fat such as butter or salad dressing. It's a matter of educating the palate to the new order. You should try it."

To her surprise, he chuckled. "Maybe I will."

Her eyes met his. He studied her rather intently. She thought she saw concern in those hazel depths. She swallowed, then said, "I'm sorry I rushed out like that."

His expression became carefully blank. "I thought it better to get it all out in the open, so there would be no misunderstanding between us."

"Thanks," she said dryly. "I appreciate your candor." She considered the situation between them and wished she'd never agreed to come there. She must have been crazy to pursue a three-year-old attraction—a purely sexual one at that.

He started to reply, but a woman called his name and dashed across the restaurant on brilliantly red high heels. Her red wool suit fitted her like a second skin. A low-neck silk shell gave an ample demonstration of her charms.

"Rafe, darling," she said, stopping by the table and lifting her face for his kiss when he stood.

He lightly brushed her lips. Lava boiled in Genny's veins. The woman's perfume bloomed around them like a rose garden. Joy, once reputed to be the most expensive perfume in the world, Genny remembered reading.

"Genny, this is Monica, Baroness Von—"

"No, no, darling, just Monica. The baron and I have parted ways." She turned heavily but expertly made-up eyes on Genny. "Lovely, darling." Then she turned back to Rafe.

As in, "Lovely to meet you"? Genny wondered. She felt completely overshadowed by the other woman, who was beautiful and worldly and assured.

"Darling, the most awful thing," the ex-baroness continued. "The front desk doesn't have a record of my reservation."

"For a good reason," Rafe said with an easy smile. "You didn't make one."

"Oh," she said. Her composure was only briefly shaken. "Well, you've caught me. I suppose I shall have to move into your place if there's nothing at the lodge."

"I have a guest." He flicked Genny a glance that singed her insides. His tone implied intimacy. "I'll call some friends with a bed and breakfast in Medford. They may be able to put you up."

"Don't bother," Monica said, her manner much cooler.

"It's no trouble." He took the woman's arm and propelled her from the table. "They're a lovely couple," he went on. "She's an artist and he's an engineer. They've made their house a showplace. You'll like it."

Genny saw a new side to Rafe—a smooth-as-butter host who knew just how to handle a difficult guest. She felt relieved that he hadn't let the woman barge in on them. Fast on the heels of that thought, she wondered why the ex-baroness had thought she could.

Had they been lovers?

She stared at her clenched hands, then forced herself to relax them. Rafe had made it clear his life was no business of hers. She would stay there until Deveraux told her it was safe to go, then she'd leave. If there was darkness inside Rafe, he'd have to find his own way out.

When he returned, she was munching on a medley of steamed vegetables. He took his seat, sighed, and picked up his fork. "One of the hazards of running a resort."

"Running into old lovers?" she inquired with a polite smile.

He checked as he reached for a roll, then smiled ruefully. "No, guests who don't know where to draw the line between business and personal."

Such as herself? Genny imagined thousands of women throwing themselves at him. "Right. That must be tough."

A scowl nicked a line between his dark brows. "You've become cynical," he said thoughtfully. "Is that a new trait?"

"Maybe." She dropped her gaze from his. "Perhaps I've learned to stop searching beneath the surface for meaning. As you pointed out, often there isn't anything else."

The roll crumbled into pieces in his hand. "I never meant to hurt you," he told her huskily.

"Your intent is plain to me . . . now. You don't have to worry that I'll read more into it than is there."

He resumed his meal without speaking. When she glanced at him, she saw the darkness for a second before he blinked and said, "Good. We should be able to get along until this is over."

Rafe observed each person as Genny called off the name. In addition to the fifteen guests and Genny, he and Bill were also going on the hike. He'd decided to tag along at the last minute.

A bit of heat crept into his neck. Okay, he'd decided to go when he saw Monica hanging out at the lodge, dressed in a designer ski outfit that had never touched the snow. The pesky woman had met friends and joined them in their suite at the lodge.

He cursed silently. Just what he needed—more complications in his life.

"Okay," Genny's call broke into his thoughts. "We're ready to go. I'll set the pace. Bill will bring up the rear. Any questions? Everyone has a lunch?"

Rafe hadn't had time to get a lunch made up, but he'd stuck a couple of candy bars in his pocket. He rolled his shoulders and felt the restraining straps of the back holster. Not that he thought he'd need a gun, but it was better to be prepared.

The hikers set out on the snowy trail. A snowmobile with a drag attached had been over the path to pack the snow. It made walking a lot easier.

He returned to the news that had caused him a sleepless night. Deveraux had found tracks in the snow yesterday. They'd come from over the ridge, not the resort. The prints had disappeared into several others at the head of a cross-country ski trail. It could mean something...or nothing.

No use getting paranoid. Now that things were straight between him and Genny, he could concentrate on the job at hand.

They tramped along for more than an hour, stopping twice to rest briefly. At noon, they arrived at a large hiking shelter. Bill unlocked the door. The group went inside.

The air inside the cabin seemed colder than the air outside. Bunks rose in tiers along the walls for the backpackers who used the shelter in summer as they hiked the ridge trails. The place had a forlorn air of disuse at present.

The chill was dispelled when Bill got a roaring fire started in the pot-bellied stove. Soon hot cider was steaming in a pot. The hikers settled on the floor and unpacked their lunches. Rafe saw Genny's gaze flick to him. He stood by the door, his back against the wall, his hands shoved into his pockets.

He noticed Bill had claimed a place next to her and frowned in annoyance. Not that it was any of his business, but perhaps he should warn Genny that Bill was a flirt.

When she rose and poured a cup of cider for herself, she didn't resume her place on the floor, but came to him.

"Here," she said, holding out the cup. "You look like you need this." Her grin was open, generous, her face flushed from cold and the brisk hike.

A drowning sensation poured over him as he gazed into her eyes. He saw her raise her eyebrows as if questioning him. He hastily reached for the cup.

She sat down next to his leg, her back resting against the wall, and opened her pack. "Hmm, ham," she observed. She held it up to him. "Take it."

"I can make it until we get back."

"There's plenty." She held up another sandwich. "See?"

There was no way he could refuse without being obviously impolite. He slid down the wall and sat beside her. She picked up the cup and took a sip when he set it down.

"That was fun," she murmured around a healthy mouthful of sandwich. She chewed and swallowed. "Are there other places we can hike to in the snow?"

He nodded. "Along Moose Creek. There's a horse trail that's used in the summer. I'll have Bill check it out."

"Maybe we can look at it this afternoon or tomorrow?"

"Maybe."

She smiled at him. It was like the sun coming out. The cabin was suddenly warm and friendly, filled with the happy conversation of people having a good time. He wondered how she did that—brought life to a place. She made him think of home...of laughter....

While they ate, he was aware of her watching him. Her eyes were bright, the color of new grass. They reminded him of summer and lush meadows, wildflowers growing and deer grazing.

A lump formed in his chest. He frowned. He couldn't afford to let himself be distracted. He wouldn't fail her the way he had failed his friend three years ago.

He gave a silent sigh. She glanced at him, then smiled in that sweet way she had, her eyes like clear summer pools.

It came to him that Genny still believed in the goodness of life. He no longer did. But he'd miss her when she left.

Genny was pleasantly tired when they neared the lodge. The trip had been a success.

Bill had helped a lot in that respect. He'd told humorous stories about life in those parts and teased the women, making each feel she was special. He'd also known a lot of nature stuff, stopping occasionally to explain interesting rock formations or to identify an interesting tree specimen.

She glanced over her shoulder. Rafe was close behind her. The rest of the group was in front of her, a bit more spread out along the trail than during the earlier journey.

For a moment she let herself dwell on the life they could have together in the mountains. Rafe belonged here. He had instinctively come to the right place to heal, but he wasn't letting anyone get close.

Maybe all they had was a sexual attraction, but she sensed the painful, chilling void in him. She knew something tender and fragile in him was in danger of being snuffed out. She wanted to protect it—his humanity, or whatever *it* was.

But he had shut her out, too. Did she dare risk her heart against the wall he'd built around his?

Yes.

The answer came from deep inside her, surprising her with its ferocity. Her heart was ready to take the risk, it seemed.

"Hot chocolate on me," Rafe told the group when they arrived back at the lodge. "In the private dining room. I arranged it before we left," he told Genny.

Everyone trooped upstairs and into the room he'd indicated. The manager, a woman in her fifties, welcomed them. The cocoa was ready. So was tea and coffee. Cookies were arranged in a pyramid on a platter. Everyone dug in.

Genny circulated, asking for suggestions to improve the outing. She was pleased to find all the guests thought it had been a fun trip, just long enough to be vigorous, but not overtiring.

From the corner of her eye, she saw Rafe speak to Bill, then head for the stairs. He was probably going to his office.

Before she could follow, a guest stopped her. "Have you other hikes planned? I'd like one that was bird-oriented, to see what species winter over in the area."

"We're checking other trails," Genny told her. "I'll post a notice if any work out. The snow can be a problem."

"Oh, good. I'll tell my husband." The woman went to the table where her husband hovered over the cookies.

Genny stopped by a window and sighed, glad that her duties as social director were over for the day. She was a solitary person for the most part, although she liked people.

A man in a blue down vest came out of the lodge and stood in the snow for a second, scanning the area. Rafe. She'd recognize his tall, lithe form anywhere.

The sun picked out shades of gold in his hair and reflected off his sunglasses as he pivoted like a camera panning a long shot, taking in the details of the scene. Then he started off at a brisk walk and disappeared on the path into the woods, not the one leading to the town houses, but the one running down by the creek.

Her heart hammering, she walked to the coatrack and pulled her parka on. She tugged on her hat and mittens.

"Hey, what's the hurry?" Bill asked, coming over to her.

She barely cast him a glance. "I have to go. Thanks for your help on the trip."

"Rafe said you were to stay here until he gets back. He asked me to keep an eye on you."

"Where's he going?"

"He said he was going to check out the horse trail—"

"Darn him," she exclaimed. She hurried past the supervisor and pelted down the steps, dodging between skiers who were taking a break from the slopes. In a minute, she was following Rafe's footprints along the creek trail.

Her heart beat heavily. Remembering her training, she stopped once in the woods, took out the semiautomatic, checked the clip, then slipped it back into the tote. She was probably overreacting. She mustn't do that. She had to stay alert and keep a cool head. That was the first rule of survival in any situation. All embassy employees were trained to handle dangerous situations.

She picked up the pace, matching her footsteps to Rafe's long strides through the snow. Sometimes it was rough going. Once she sank into the crusty snow to a point past her knees. She pushed on, panting.

Don't work up a sweat, she cautioned, then realized it was too late to worry about hypothermia. She pulled the zipper down a few inches to let hot air and moisture escape.

Where was Rafe? Surely she should have caught up with him by now. Darn his long stride... and his independent ways. What if she didn't find him? What if— No, she couldn't afford to think along those lines.

Her breath labored in and out. She didn't dare call his name. That would be a dead giveaway. Oh, God!

She pressed on. Time became meaningless. The future and the past compressed into the all-important present. There was only *now,* this instant of time...speeding away....

Her body ached with cold for a while, then she no longer felt it. Her throat was raw from breathing the dry air through her mouth. It couldn't be helped. She walked faster...faster.

At last she caught a flicker of movement ahead. Leaping like a deer, she bounded over a drift of hard-packed snow that came to her hips. She spotted Rafe striding around the next bend. She bit her lip, vexed that she couldn't call out to him.

She discovered she could walk on the crust at the edge of the trail without breaking through. He couldn't. That would slow him down some. She skipped along as lightly as she could, gaining on him. If he would only look back...

Rounding the next bend in the path, she stopped abruptly. His tracks disappeared...right in the middle of the path. The hair stood up on the back of her neck.

A fall of snow and a curse came down on her. Rafe dropped out of a tree a couple of feet in front of her. Genny clutched her chest as relief wafted through her.

"What the hell do you think you're doing?" he demanded, his fists settling on his jean-clad hips. He looked ready to breathe fire and burn her to a crisp.

"Following you," she replied, just as angry. "What do you think *you're* doing, traipsing off alone like this?"

He obviously didn't think she deserved an answer. "You little fool. You could get yourself killed—"

"So could you." She returned his glare.

His chest lifted as he took a calming breath. "So Devereaux told you about the tracks." He glanced down the trail they were following. "I thought the guy might have come this way, then joined the cross-country trail near the Moosehead and come up over the ridge toward the town houses."

"What tracks?" The agent hadn't told her about any tracks. She realized someone could have been in the woods the other day, that the suspicious bush might not have been the product of an overactive imagination.

Rafe's eyes narrowed as he took in her expression. "You didn't know," he accurately guessed. "But you saw something in the woods...again. Why the hell didn't you report it?"

"I thought I was being paranoid. It was just a bush or a shadow...." She tried to remember exactly what she thought she'd seen, but the details were blurry now.

Rafe muttered a distinct curse. "Come on. We'd better get out of here." He paused, then pointed down the trail. "We'll go to the Moosehead, cut through the parking lot and return on the road. The traffic will be heavy with skiers going back to town."

He set off down the trail with an admonition for her to stay close. That was something he didn't have to worry about. She wasn't about to let him get more than two feet in front of her.

They were alone out here. No one knew where they were, except Bill, and he knew of no reason to report their whereabouts. She realized she should have found Deveraux and told him that Rafe was exploring the trail on his own.

Noting Rafe was pulling ahead of her, she forced herself to pick up the pace. The earlier surge of adrenaline was gone, and it was harder to walk. The clinging snow seemed to hinder her every step.

They walked at a fast clip for another half hour. Finally she saw the roof of the Moosehead Bar and Grill through the bare branches of the poplars. Rafe guided them through the parking lot, which was filling with vehicles loaded with ski equipment as the younger crowd stopped to warm up and chat before going home.

Genny followed Rafe to the left side of the road and started uphill, facing traffic. She sighed in relief and realized how tense she'd been for the past hour.

A soak in the hot tub would feel good. Her hands and feet were partly numb, yet aching, too. The temperature was dropping rapidly as the day drew to a close.

She glanced at Rafe's broad back in front of her. She wished they were going home, that they were married and this was the end of the workday for them, that soon they'd be in the hot tub, the world shut out....

Pulling herself back from useless longing, she trudged along without speaking. Rafe turned onto the last steep-hill path to the town houses. A shiver of dread went through her. She didn't like the area through here. The dense woods made her feel uneasy.

They reached the railroad ties that formed steps in the very steep section. The meadow opened, long and narrow to each side of them. This was where the man had motioned for her to come to him. She glanced all around.

"Nervous?"

She reddened at Rafe's amused tone. "Yes."

"Me, too." He gave her a sardonic grin.

There wasn't a nervous bone in his body. She resented being teased. "Then why did you take off on your own? Why not send Deveraux? He's paid to be a hero."

"This is my domain," Rafe informed her. "The security of the resort is my responsibility."

He started off, then stopped when he realized she wasn't staying right on his heels. "Keep up," he ordered.

"I can't. My feet are numb."

He scowled, as if the chill factor were her fault, but he let her take the lead. As they started off again, a flurry of noise beat above them. He grabbed Genny and pulled her behind him.

An owl and several jays took off, screeching imprecations on the humans below. Rafe scanned the woods for shadows that didn't move or ones that moved too much.

A hail sounded in the woods to their left. Deveraux came into sight. "Yo," he called.

Rafe stepped away from Genny. "What the hell are you doing off the trail? A person could get shot sneaking around in the woods like that."

"Sorry. I was following some tracks."

"Tracks? Whose?"

"I'm not sure. Someone has been running around in the woods. The local police are bringing in dogs. The sheriff said there was a snow shack up in the woods. We'll check it out." The agent glanced at Genny and nodded a greeting.

"Do you think the tracks belong to the mercenary?" she asked.

Rafe thought of someone harming her. A wild anger ran over him. He calmed it. He'd better get her home right away.

Deveraux shrugged. "It could have been someone from the resort. People get lost in the strangest places."

Rafe felt Genny shiver as the cold settled around them like an invisible shroud. He realized she must be exhausted. She'd been hiking through the snow for hours. It did strange things to him to know she'd been concerned enough to follow him, obviously worried he might be in danger because of her.

"We'd better go in," he said, his voice unintentionally gruff. "Genny's cold. She's had a long day."

"A soak in the hot tub will take the chill out," the agent replied with an envious grin. "Stay in the house tonight. I'll let you know if we find anything at the snow cabin."

"Thanks."

The agent passed them and was soon out of sight. Rafe saw Genny's hands tremble as she zipped her parka tighter. She stuck them in her pockets. He found her mittens, handed them to her and urged her up the trail. She was taking a chill.

They reached the town houses...the last building...the ten steps. He heard her count them as they went up. Yes, definitely signs of hypothermia. The body could take only so much.

At last he opened the door and urged her inside the warm house. He was glad he'd left the thermostat up.

"I can do that," she remonstrated when he started stripping her coat and hat off.

"I'll help."

He pushed her down onto the stairs and removed her hiking boots. When he took off her socks, her feet were mottled white with a blue tinge around her toes. He cursed under his breath. He rubbed her feet gently. No indications of severe frostbite, thank goodness.

"I knew the tenderness was still in you," she told him.

"Hush," he said.

"I like your voice—all husky and soft, yet sort of rough and growly. I used to listen for you, there in the desert."

He yanked her sweater off and started on her shirt. The telephone rang. "Get out of your things and into the tub," he ordered, heading for the wall phone.

While he answered, she disappeared up the stairs. "Hello?" he snapped into the receiver.

"Rafe?" It was his sister.

"Hello, Rachel," he said in a calmer tone.

"What's wrong?" she asked. They had always been close, quick to catch on to nuances in the other's voice.

"Nothing. I, uh, just got in from checking out some trails. Our guests like to hike in the snow, it seems."

"Oh. Well, I wanted to check with you on your plans for Christmas. I just spoke to Mom. She and Dad won't get in until Christmas Eve."

"An international crisis, no doubt," he said dryly.

"Of course. They have to attend a special opera performance with the Queen of England."

"Hmm, I suppose the queen does have priority." They laughed in unison. The conversation was reminiscent of others they'd had through the years. During their growing years, it hadn't always seemed humorous.

"So. When are *you* going to arrive?"

Rafe hesitated when Genny appeared on the stairs. She had on a robe and house slippers. She glanced at him once, then went into the hall on the way to his bedroom. In a minute, he heard the sound of the spa motor come on.

"Rafe?"

"I'm thinking," he said. "Listen, sis, something has come up here. I might not be able to make it this year."

"Not at all?"

Her disappointment rang clearly through the line. They'd always been there for each other, especially at special times. Of course, Rachel had a family of her own to keep her company now.

The bleakness of the empty town house during holidays past swept into his consciousness. "I... there's a problem. I have a houseguest."

"Bring her," his sister retorted.

"How do you know the guest is a *her?*" He was stalling for time. He'd have to check with Deveraux to see what the plan was.

"I have this feeling. It is, isn't it?"

"Yes," he admitted. He pictured Genny at the ranch. She'd like it there. She'd fit in. His nephew and niece would love her.

Another picture came to him. Genny with the sun on her hair, sitting in a grassy meadow, a child in her lap. He was there, too. With them. His family.

From a place deep within—he didn't know where—came the idea of having a home of his own, one filled with love like his sister had found. A home... a wife... children—

A shudder went through him. He couldn't let himself be distracted by things that would never be. Desire for a woman could make a man careless...like he'd been when Tom was killed. His desire for Genny had made him forget his duties.

"So bring her," Rachel ordered.

He took a breath. "It isn't that simple. Genny—"

"Genny?" his sister broke in. "Genny? Isn't that the name of the woman—" She stopped, as if realizing she'd said too much.

"Yes." He spoke abruptly, wanting to put an end to that line of questioning.

Rachel was the only person who knew the truth about the past. In a moment of intense loneliness, he'd told her the story.

Ever loyal to him, she'd tried to convince him it wasn't his fault, but he knew it was. He should have been more alert. He should have pushed the security guards to inspect the embassy vehicles more carefully.

It was too late to think about the past. He had the present to think of. And Genny to protect. If anything happened to her...

"I'll let you know, okay?"

"Sure," Rachel said. Her concern for him came clearly through the line. "Call me." She hesitated. "There's one other thing. It was sort of odd. Dad asked me a month or two ago if I thought you'd ever been in love."

Every cell in his body snapped to attention. "What did you say?" he finally asked.

"I told him you had. About three years ago." There was a taut silence. "I'm sorry if I spoke out of turn."

Rafe cursed to himself. To his sister, he said, "It's okay. Listen, I've got to go. I'll talk to you later."

They said goodbye and hung up. He stayed where he was for a moment, lost in thought, wondering why his father was suddenly concerned about his love life. And what the connection to Genny was.

He went to his room to check on his guest. She opened her eyes when he appeared at the door.

She smiled sleepily. "About time," she grumbled, clearly expecting him to join her.

He watched her for a moment. She had on a bathing suit, he noted. Her eyes were dark, swept by emotions he didn't want to acknowledge...and couldn't ignore. "I wasn't coming in."

"I want you to," she said.

He closed his eyes against needs he didn't want to feel. He knew he should resist, but the days...weeks... months...without her had been too long. "All right."

"Shall I help you?" she offered.

He shook his head and grimly concentrated on the task of undressing. She needed him. It was in her eyes. That's all he could think of at the moment. He finished and eased into the spa.

She touched him. "This feels like a dream," she whispered. "Am I dreaming?"

Chapter Eight

"Does it matter?" Rafe asked. Life was full of dreams, and just as full of nightmares. Sometimes it was hard to tell where one started and the other stopped.

She touched his thigh, then his abdomen, then his chest as he sank into the water. Suddenly he was warm... all over.

He moved close to her, then lifted her onto his lap. Using the gentlest touch he could, he raised her chin and looked into her troubled gaze. "What is it?"

She shook her head. "I was so afraid," she whispered. "You shouldn't go out alone. Don't do it again. Promise me."

"Shh," he quietened her. He guided her head to his shoulder. "I don't make promises."

"Why?" she cried softly. "Why?"

Rafe closed his eyes. He'd taken an oath to protect his government and its people, to carry out his missions faithfully and honorably. He'd failed. He'd let himself get caught up in a magic he couldn't resist. He'd made promises once. Never again.

"There are no guarantees in life," he said.

She slumped against him, her anxiety subsiding. "No, but there are other things."

He held Genny closer. A feeling—he couldn't define it—grew in his chest. It pushed against his insides, demanding space, hurting in its intensity. A violent shudder went through him, and he pressed his face into her hair.

She smelled of life, Genny did.

Rage burned momentarily in him that she had been forced into danger by a madman who cared nothing for life. The mercenary would kill her without one twinge of a conscience.

The world would be the loser if she were gone.

The fury abated as she began to stroke along his shoulder with one hand. She clasped his neck with the other, her thumb stroking under his jaw.

He closed his eyes. Her touch spread warmth, thawing places in him that the steam from the spa couldn't penetrate. He was fully aroused, but the ache was pleasant for a change, not cold, not hurting, not filled with desire he knew would never be slaked.

With danger all around, he knew it was normal to seek an affirmation of life. Sex, with its possibility of creation, was the typical answer to that need.

Making love with her brought its own kind of danger. He let himself acknowledge it. Her warmth could dissolve the most solid of glaciers. And then what? He didn't know.

Another shudder went through him. Whatever the cost, he knew he wouldn't stop if she wanted him to make love to her. It had gone beyond his control. The need for her was greater than his need for survival.

He ran a hand down her hair, learning the silky feel of it through his skin. The upper layer was cool. When he ran his fingers into the shining strands, he found the warmth again.

She moved her hand down from his shoulder and rubbed the hair on his chest. Then she settled her head against his shoulder and rested in his arms with a contented sigh.

For now, for both of them, there was only them—a man and a woman...and the warmth...the incredible warmth.

Genny snuggled against the wonderfully hard length of him and felt a surge of pure satisfaction.

"I love it here," she whispered. "I love the mountains and the river with its intriguing name. The Rogue. You belong to it, to this land. How did you find this place?"

"I think of it as my inheritance," he admitted. "My early years were spent in boarding school or following my parents to different diplomatic posts. My uncle had a ranch near Medford. Since he never married, my sister and I inherited it. It was too small to be profitable, and too close to town. We sold it and bought the resort. I knew I'd come back here someday."

"To raise a family?" she suggested softly.

"Actually, to retire. I've never thought much about having a family. Are you warm now?"

"Yes." She gazed at him, enchanted all over again, the way she'd been when they first met. "You'd be a wonderful father. Remember the goatherd's daughter and the thorn you removed from her foot? I'd want a man like that for my children."

"Don't," he warned. "This is only for the moment."

"Haven't you ever wanted anyone to share life with you?" she couldn't help but ask.

"No."

He looked so grim, she didn't pursue the topic. Perhaps some other time he would tell her why. For this moment she was content to be with him. Danger seemed far away.

The chill had completely left her. In its place came a growing awareness. There was a destiny between them that had never been fulfilled. Other events had interceded. But now... She knew she wouldn't pull back this time. Neither would he.

If she had only a few days here with him, she would take all the memories she could. She stroked his firm jaw. "Tell me what you like."

That drew a quick, sharp chuckle. He laid her hand against his chest. "I doubt there's anything you could do that would displease me. Unless you said no."

"I'm not going to do that. I've wanted you too long."

"Hasn't anyone taught you coquetry?"

"I didn't think it necessary between us." She raised herself so she could look into his eyes. "Do you?"

"No."

He lifted her then and placed her astride his lap as he had that other time. With hands on her hips, he guided her against him and moved his hips. She caught her bottom lip between her teeth as tumultuous sensation flooded her. They fit so snugly, so perfectly together.

"Rafe," she whispered, knowing only joy at that moment.

"Is this what you wanted?"

"Oh, yes!"

"You respond so beautifully. It makes a man feel..."

She waited for the rest, but he didn't finish the thought. Instead he clasped her hips and guided her in erotic movements that delighted her.

The languid contentment fled. Raging excitement leapt through her blood, spreading outward to every part of her. This was right. She knew it.

If only he would let himself see it, too.

No, she wasn't going to think of that. There was only the moment and the beauty of their coming together the way they should have three years ago. Beyond that, she couldn't think.

When he lifted her clear of the churning water, peeled the swimsuit from her and bent forward to kiss her breast, she nearly came apart in his hands. He ran his tongue over her nipple again and again until it drew into a tight bud.

He kissed a line up her chest, then her neck and then her lips. She sighed and opened to him. He took possession of her mouth, stroking and enticing her to join in the love play.

She did so gladly, moving her tongue against his in the same rhythm that their bodies glided against each other. When he left her mouth, he nipped at her neck. With his roaming hands, he found a ticklish spot. She laughed and squirmed. He kissed her again.

And suddenly it wasn't play, but serious. She caught her breath as pressure built and built. He paused for a second, then with a low sound in the back of his throat, he pulled her tighter against his hips and encouraged her to counter his movements with her own.

"Rafe, I...it's..."

"I know. Let it happen. I want you to let go."

She closed her eyes and strained against him, unable to stop the tide of sensation, the one need that overtook all others.

"That's right," he coaxed. "Come to me. Move with me."

She was trembling. Wave after wave of tremors shook her to her very foundation. The world shifted, expanded... contracted... exploded... disappeared.

He held her, kissing her forehead, her temple, while she slumped against him. She was weak, her passion spent in a wild moment of total release.

"Don't let go," she whispered. Even her voice was weary. She'd drown if he released her.

"I won't."

She heard the promise in the words and wondered if he'd realized he'd given it. "Take me to bed," she pleaded.

"All right." His voice was the desert wind, so soft, reaching so deeply within her, calling her soul to his.

"Your bed," she added, in case he didn't understand.

"I know." His laughter was brief, a rueful note, even a touch of sadness under the rough melody of his passion.

He rose from the swirling, steaming water and placed her on the tiles. Picking up a towel, he dried her gently, himself more hastily. He was still hard with desire, his phallus rising from its curling nest of dark blond hair like a pagan symbol of life.

Life. He was life to her—the meaning, the depth and the scope of all it could be. Without him, she was empty inside. She needed him to fill her....

She blinked the sudden sting of tears from her eyes. This wasn't the time for them. She knew he would hate it if she cried now, although he would hold her and comfort her.

"Hurry," she said.

After flipping the towel over his head, he wiped it along his back, then tossed it aside. Never taking his eyes from hers, he lifted her, then carried her to his bed.

Dropping her feet to the carpet, he used his free hand to sweep the covers back. For a second the intensity returned to his expression along with all those other emotions she couldn't identify. She knew she had to dispel them before he retreated from her.

The world spun as he grabbed her up, placed a knee on the bed, then fell onto it, pinning her under his greater weight. The evidence of his passion throbbed impatiently against her. They had this. For now, he was hers.

She laughed.

"God, your laughter," he whispered, burying his face in her hair. "It could turn the blackest night into day. Sometimes it was all I had—" He stopped, as if he'd said too much.

She felt his despair. "Don't." She cupped his precious face between her hands. "Let's find the light together."

Rafe wanted to tell her there was no light, but he couldn't. Looking into her eyes, he saw the promise of all the good things he once thought life had to offer.

He had to be careful. He could be swept into her magic and forget that danger lurked right outside.

She moved under him, drawing him back into her golden web of life, into her belief in the goodness of others. He couldn't let her go, not yet. Passion was okay. He could handle passion. He'd had other women and it had been okay. It would be all right this time, too.

He eased his weight to one side, freeing one hand to move and explore her silky body. Her breast was smooth, a firm globe that swelled against his palm, inviting him to further intimacy. He liked the hard button of her nipple centered in his hand. When he stroked back and forth, she arched upward.

Once, as a kid on his uncle's ranch, he'd overheard a couple of cowboys talking. "You can tell a woman wants you," one of them had stated wisely, "when she comes up to meet you."

The full meaning of that observation came home to him with Genny. She thrust forward, her sweet body rising to meet each caress of his, a demand in the low sound she made.

It blew his control all to hell.

A tremor of need rushed through him. He left her breast and stroked down her slender rib cage, over her waist, the womanly flare of her hips. He cupped the delicate feminine mound and let his fingers slide into the intimate valley between her thighs.

She was hot and wet and ready. The incredible smoothness of her intrigued him. He stroked that smooth, moist place for a minute, pleasuring her as well as himself.

At last, he could take no more. He lifted, moved both his legs between hers and sought the haven he both dreaded and desired.

Biting back a groan, he positioned himself and began the slow plunge into her... into warmth. It was like coming home.

He felt her arch beneath him. She came up to him, rising to meet his downward thrust, drawing him into her, taking him as deep as he could go.

She gave a shaky sigh, held him tightly with her arms clasped around his neck for a minute, then began to caress his back. When she reached his hips, she pressed against him, urging him to move.

The warmth reached up to him. It enclosed him, and he was surrounded by her. Genny. As open and generous with her passion as with her smiles.

Genny. Being in her was like being in the heart of the sun. Radiant. Life-giving.

Melting. He was melting. He didn't care. Tomorrow, he might, but not now. Now there was all this warmth, flowing from her to him . . . a river of light between them.

"You make me forget," he murmured. They were safe for the moment. It was okay to have this. Tomorrow he'd have to be on guard, but for now, he would take all the night could give.

"Forget what?" she asked. She kissed his ear, then his neck. She bit him, then kissed the spot, then licked it.

He felt her hips moving against him, seeking satisfaction. With trembling fingers, he stroked the smooth bud of passion until she forgot her question. He forgot it, too.

There was *this*. There was *now*. It was enough.

The sun exploded, and he was consumed in its fire, in Genny's fire. He felt her come apart in his hands. Just for a second, he sensed the terrible pain, then it, too, was gone, and there was only the haven of fulfillment, the sweet honey of her body flowing over him as he poured his seed into her.

He knew he'd forgotten something . . . something important . . . but it went out of his mind.

There was *now*. There was *this*. It would have to be enough.

Genny lay still, suspended in time, in space, in his arms. Her breathing slowed to deep, contented sighs. The wild gallop of her blood calmed to a lazy, meandering pace.

"Mmm," she murmured, still not sure she hadn't dreamed the past hour. She'd lived a lifetime in those tumultuous moments. She'd learned what passion really meant.

Now there was only this vast luxury of lying there with her love. Minutes passed, floating over them like a warm desert breeze. Still he held her.

She flexed her thighs, enjoying the sensuous weight of Rafe on her and ran her hands over him. When he started to move, she clutched him to her, not wanting the magical connection broken.

"Stay," she said.

"I'm too heavy for you."

"You feel wonderful." She kissed along his collarbone and licked the salty taste from his skin.

"If I stay..." he warned.

Enchanted, she wondered what would happen. Would he make love to her again? Muscles clenched inside her at the thought. She felt him there, not rigid now, but not exactly spent, either.

"Rafe?"

He groaned and turned his face to her. His mouth sought hers. "See what you've done?" he whispered against her lips. "I want you again. I knew once wouldn't be enough."

"I'm here," she said simply.

When he raised himself over her, she gazed up at him in open adoration. He closed his eyes. "Don't."

"Rafe, I lo—"

His mouth stopped her confession. But he couldn't kiss her forever, she reasoned with some tiny part of her mind, and then she would tell him...and make him listen to her.

Time was fleeting, and life could be sweet, so sweet, if they were together. Three years wasted! But no more...

Her thoughts went spinning out of control as he moved inside her again. When he slipped a hand between them and caressed her to full passion once more, she forgot the words. None were needed.

She returned his kisses with every ounce of love she had. It seemed to pour out of her, erupting from some cataclysmic place deep inside, burning her, burning him with her fire.

"You're like the sun," he panted, holding her head between his hands and kissing her. "You give... light. And life. You're so warm. It's cold out here. Better that way...but..."

"It's all right," she whispered, offering comfort, but not understanding his words.

He sounded so sad, so full of grief. She didn't know what to say. Making love to her seemed to hurt him in ways she couldn't comprehend.

"We can be together," she assured him. "We don't have to be lonely, to stay in the cold."

"You don't know." He closed his eyes and moved his hands over her, finding those smooth vortexes of passion, exciting her to blind ecstasy. "You...don't...know."

She held him against her breasts. She lifted her knees high to take him deeper, but she knew he was trying to put distance between them, even now, at this moment of joining. She felt the sadness. She knew the cold he spoke of.

"Don't go," she cried.

"Shh," he said. "I'm here. I won't leave. I couldn't."

But she knew, even as he caressed her more fiercely, even as the passion burst over them and shattered the present, she knew he was withdrawing.

"Liar," she said, tossing the word back to him as he'd once tossed it to her.

He didn't deny it.

* * *

Rafe slept. He woke with Genny in his arms. Actually, she was sort of draped over him, her head on his chest, an arm and leg flung across him. The T-shirt he'd tucked between her legs was scrunched between their thighs.

An alarm went off inside him. He remembered the important thing he'd forgotten during their passionate sessions—a thing he'd never forgotten before in his life.

Protection. He'd forgotten to use a condom. How could he have forgotten? He never forgot things...never! Except when she was around. Then he forgot everything.

Restless now, he eased away from her. She stirred and turned over, moving from him and onto her side of the bed. He remembered he hadn't let her go last night.

When she'd started to rise, to leave him, he'd held her tighter, not wanting to break the contact.

"I need something to sleep in," she'd murmured drowsily.

"You have me," he'd told her. "I'll keep you warm."

The moment came back to him. The tenderness. The incredible tenderness he'd felt for her... for this woman. This Genevieve McBride. He'd never felt that for anyone before.

Was that love?

When he was sure she was settled, he rose from the bed. He slipped into deck shoes and pulled on a velour robe his sister had given him for Christmas years ago. He rarely wore it.

In the kitchen, he put on the coffee, then looked at the stairs. He turned and glanced out the window. Stars were still visible, but the sky was brightening to the east. Another hour before the gray light of dawn. He looked toward the stairs.

Did she have protection? It wouldn't hurt to check. Then he wouldn't have to spend the next couple of hours wondering.

He didn't get farther than halfway up the oak stairs before he turned and came back down. He couldn't go rummaging through her things. An odd sense of honor wouldn't let him.

The coffeemaker gurgled one last time. He poured a cup and took it to the table. He sat in the dark and watched the day pour over the eastern horizon in gentle infusions of light. He was still there when Genny came in.

She was wearing her jeans and one of his sweatshirts, the sleeves rolled up several times. Socks covered her feet.

"Hi," she said. Her face was washed, her hair combed. She looked as fresh as the dawn.

She didn't seem to notice his frown. Instead she came over and stopped beside him. Dropping her arms over his shoulders, she bent and kissed his ear, then nibbled delicately on his earlobe.

"I used one of your toothbrushes," she murmured, and kissed the corner of his mouth. "Was that okay?"

"Yeah, sure."

The cold shifted around inside him, barely staying ahead of her concentrated warmth. Her skin still faintly smelled of that sleepy essence a person has when waking up. She'd washed, but he detected the musky scent of their lovemaking lingering like an aura around her. Or maybe he imagined it.

He turned his head from her and tried to focus his mind on the things they needed to discuss.

She pressed a last kiss on his cheek and went to get a cup of coffee. While she got out eggs and cheese and started the toast, he tried to think of how to bring up the subject.

"Bacon?" she called.

"Uh, yes."

She smiled at him, then opened the refrigerator, removed the bacon and put several slices in the microwave oven.

It wasn't until the meal was on the table that he cleared his throat, determined to broach the problem.

"Last night..." he began, then hesitated.

"Was wonderful." She completed the sentence. With an impish twinkle, she asked solemnly, "Was it as good for you as it was for me?" She lifted her fork.

He swallowed the bite of omelet and reached inside for the anger. Anger was a safe emotion. It didn't commit a man to anything. "Sex is always good," he stated bluntly.

For a second, the brightness in her eyes dimmed, then she nodded and gave him another smile. "Yes."

"There's one thing— I, uh, didn't use anything. Did you?"

She looked totally perplexed.

"You can't be that naive," he growled. "I didn't use a condom. I forgot."

"I forgot, too. I guess we were both caught up in the moment." Thoughtful now, she chewed a bite of toast and stared at the crescent of light appearing over the mountains. "Are you angry?"

"Yes." He bit a piece of bacon in two. "You could be pregnant," he snarled at her, wondering what it would take to get through to her that this was a disaster.

Her dreamy look disappeared. "We're right back where we were before we made love—"

"Had sex."

"Made love."

"Or made a baby," he added harshly.

Genny returned his glare. Then she sighed and put her fork down. "It's a little late for recriminations, isn't it?"

The bleak darkness returned to his eyes as the fire of anger burned out. She felt the loss as an answering, dark chasm inside.

"Yes," he agreed grimly.

"Then there's nothing more to say." She clenched her napkin, finding it difficult to go on. What had been beautiful and so very right for her was a disaster to him. She could almost hate him for taking that away from her.

"We have to talk, whether you want to or not."

"Fine. I love you. What are you going to do about it?"

She watched a muscle jump in his cheek as he clenched his jaw again. He pushed the chair back and stood. "Not a damn thing. I never asked for it. I don't want it."

"You got it, anyway," she said to his retreating back.

He stopped by the kitchen counter and banged his fist down on the sandstone-colored surface. "It— You don't understand."

"Understand what?" With trembling fingers, she picked up a toast half and nibbled at it.

"Last night. It was the danger. It heightens feelings, makes you do things you wouldn't do normally."

"Things like making love?" She swallowed the toast down with orange juice. It felt like a rock in her stomach.

"Sex," he said doggedly, "things like sex."

"Comradeship of the foxhole? I don't think so."

"I do."

She rose and went to him. Laying a hand on his arm, she softly reminded him, "I wanted you long before yesterday. I've wanted you for almost three years. It was the same for you."

His face hardened. The coldness returned to his eyes. "Now we've had each other. As far as I'm concerned, that's the end of it."

"What if we have a child?"

The bones seemed to stand out in his face. She was frightened by the riffle of emotion that went through him and disappeared like a pebble in a pond.

"There won't be a child." He walked away.

She returned to the table. The sun was over the horizon now. Fresh snow had fallen during the night. The landscape looked like a Christmas postcard. But cold. So cold.

Rafe left a few minutes later without speaking to her. He locked the door behind him and went down the path. It was Monday, she remembered. Just another day in paradise.

She couldn't smile at the attempt at humor. Life wasn't funny at the moment. To go from ecstasy to despair in less than twenty-four hours was too much.

For most of the morning she simply sat and looked out the windows, not thinking, not even feeling very much...well, maybe a twinge of intense regret once in a while. She wasn't sure what she regretted—meeting Rafe, coming here, or making love.

She sighed, feeling all tangled inside. At last, she put the dishes away, cleaned the kitchen, then showered and dressed herself. It was time to get on with her duties.

At the lodge, the children, nine of them ranging in age from eight to eleven, were ready to go. The leader of the expedition was a bird-watcher Val had recommended. He was going to take the group on a nature hike to a marshy area where Canadian geese wintered over.

As part of the package, the kids got lunch when they returned and then a story. Genny had picked out an adventure book to read aloud during "quiet time."

Pulling her knit cap down over her ears, she walked along behind the five boys and four girls to make sure no one got left behind on the trail. She glanced back often, aware that the group was being followed.

Deveraux was keeping an eye on her.

The police dogs had located the cabin where the mercenary had stayed. Ashes in the hearth and footprints in the snow had confirmed his use of the place. And snowmobile tracks. He'd left, taking everything with him. The police had decided he'd gotten scared off now that he knew they were on to him.

Genny doubted that. So did Deveraux, although in his usual, tight-lipped way, he wasn't talking. However, he was still there.

At the marshy pond, the expert pointed out many species of waterfowl. It was funny to watch them land on the ice, their bodies skidding, their wings beating the air as they tried to stop. Sometimes they crashed into other birds, sending them sprawling and honking across the ice. The kids suppressed their laughter with hands over their mouths.

Going back to the lodge, Genny was grateful it had been a good trip. She smiled as one ten-year-old boy lingered until he was just in front of one of the girls. The two had crushes on each other. She'd seen their eyes meet often on the hike, then skip away, embarrassed to be caught looking.

She would love to have a child like either of those. Rafe's son or daughter. If she were pregnant, she'd keep the child, of course. Rafe would have to make his own decision about his part in the child's life.

When they arrived at the lodge, she saw him sitting at the window in the restaurant. His eyes met hers through the glass. She waved. After a heartbeat, he waved back.

She noticed he had his parka with him. He'd been following them. She glanced around. There was the agent. An odd procession they must have made, going down to the marsh, her and the expert and the kids, then two silent, watchful men, each alone, each preferring life that way.

Chapter Nine

Rafe looked at the photos. They were part of a new ad campaign he and Val were planning. The pictures were glossy—filled with the "beautiful people" having fun at the resort.

"I don't like 'em," he said, tossing a photo of a glamorous model smiling at the camera from a ski-lift chair back onto the pile of similar scenes.

The model's designer outfit was hot pink with paisley swirls in green and gold. It would set a person back a cool thousand to buy it. That price didn't include skis and poles and boots, in case a person actually wanted to ski.

Val glanced at her watch. "I've got to have some lunch. I'm starved," she grumbled.

He checked the time. Almost three. "Let's go upstairs. I'll buy," he added at the frown on his assistant's face.

She grinned. "You've got a deal."

"Bring the file. We'll go through the pics again."

She gathered the glossy photos into a neat stack and put them in the file folder. Rafe held the door for her, then followed her out of her office and up the steps.

"Hi, y'all," the waitress said when they appeared. She was a tall, leggy Texan from Amarillo with a wild mane of blondish hair. Her name was Maria Janina, but she preferred to be called M.J. "Your table is taken, but there's another close by. Okay?"

Rafe nodded and smiled. He automatically took in the scene, noting areas that needed attention. The carpet took a beating from people clomping in with snow on their boots, but it was supposed to be vacuumed several times a day and cleaned every week.

"Carpet needs to be seen to," Valerie remarked. "I'll tell the dining room manager."

"Good." He crossed that item off his list. He'd made a wise choice in Val. She was as sharp-eyed as a hawk and took as great a care with the running of the resort as he did.

They were seated at a table for four near his usual place. After they ordered, he opened the file and looked at the pictures again. "What's wrong with these damn pictures?"

Val shook her head. "They look great to me—glamorous people having fun in the snow. It's similar to what we did last year and the year before... with great success, I might add."

"Yeah, right."

"Look, there's Genny." Val leaned toward the wide expanse of window and peered down toward the entrance of the lodge.

A stone seemed to drop inside him from some great height. He glanced out the window. His pulse went to Mach 1 speed in a single leap. Yes, there was Genny, looking like the Pied Piper with a string of children following her.

The story hour was apparently over. He watched the group as they said goodbye and headed off with their parents and siblings.

Finally, Genny stood alone. Her parka and jeans weren't name brands, yet he thought she looked better than the models in the photos. She looked *real.* Like a person you would want for a friend. Like a person you could trust.

"That's it," he said.

Val gave him a curious look.

"Trust," he said, mulling the idea over. "Friendship." He thought of the way the children had lingered with her, the way their parents had stayed to talk to her. "Family values."

"Beg pardon?"

He gestured toward the file folder. "These aren't people the average person would know. Glamour is fine. It has its place. However, people take vacations with their families."

"I get it," Val said. "The family that skis together stays together."

"Something like that... but more..." He stared at the winter scene—the lofty peaks with their crown of snow, the skiers on the hill, the families heading for the chair lifts. And Genny.

Over to the side of the entrance door, Deveraux was shoveling snow out of the way, keeping the path clear. Rafe noticed the man watching Genny as he worked. His earlier anger returned.

When he'd realized the agent wasn't going to follow Genny and the group on the nature hike, he'd grabbed his parka and trailed along behind them to keep an eye on her. He'd been worried that she might wander off by herself.

She was so damn trusting, she couldn't imagine one human hurting another. He could. He'd seen man's humanity toward his fellow beings. It was the pits.

A mercenary was the most dangerous kind of predator. He wasn't desperate. He wasn't driven by deep-seated convictions. In fact, it was doubtful he had compulsions of any kind.

The man was cold, cunning, and without conscience. He set his goal and worked methodically toward it, taking the precautions of a demolition squad in destroying a building. He'd watch out for himself first. If he failed, he'd lay low and try again. There was always another day.

Rafe felt the chill creep down his spine. Damn her uncle for getting her into this mess! Why couldn't the ambassador have asked someone else to do that translation?

And Deveraux, he added, his fury growing. Genny was in danger, and all the intelligence department could come up with was to set her up as a target.

"Rafe?"

It took him a second to retreat from the anger. "Yeah?"

"You looked so fierce. Is something wrong?"

He sighed, then glanced back out the window where Genny stood watching the skiers dash down the mountain. He saw Bill speak to Deveraux and amble over to Genny.

She retrieved a notepad from her pocket, and they consulted over it for several minutes. Jealousy leapt to blazing life in Rafe. Genny was *his*.

"Nothing's wrong," he finally said.

"It's Genny, isn't it?" Val asked softly. Her eyes widened as if she'd just made a discovery. "You're in love with her."

"No—"

"I suspected...and then you were so cold to her, I thought I must be wrong. But she was staying with you...." Val's voice trailed off. She looked at him in open speculation.

Rafe felt the heat rise from deep inside and climb into his face. He probably looked like a kid with a crush. "It's not what you think," he started to explain, then stopped. He couldn't begin to explain what it was between them. He didn't know himself.

"Oh?" Val looked interested.

"She's here to recuperate. She was ill, in the hospital." His explanation sounded lame. "She's a friend of the family. My father and her uncle..."

He frowned. Those two were in cahoots—his relative and hers. They'd sent her to him, knowing he didn't want her...couldn't have her. But the wanting...the need for her. It drove him wild. He didn't deserve... Ah, God, how did life get so complicated?

Last night...touching her...like touching the sun. Warm. She was so damn warm. For a few hours it had felt so damn good.

Looking out the window, he saw Deveraux put his shovel down and walk over to Genny and the maintenance supervisor. Rafe felt the coldness return like a wall of ice falling on him.

There was reality. A madman was on the loose. Genny was in danger. Why the hell hadn't Deveraux stuck with her on that hike?

The man had followed along, but not until Rafe had set

out behind them. He'd have a word with the agent... maybe the man's supervisor back at headquarters. He still had some influence.

"You've known her for a long time?"

"Yes," he murmured. "A long time."

"And loved her for years," she concluded. Her smile was sad. "It's hell on the heart, isn't it?"

He followed Val's gaze to the three people standing in the snow. Longing was evident in her eyes as she watched Genny, Bill and Deveraux. "Bill," he said, understanding dawning.

Val's cheeks pinkened. She suddenly looked confused and younger than her years. He'd worked with her for three years without once thinking about her hopes and feelings, certainly he hadn't thought about her love life.

"Does he—?"

"No," she said, giving her head a quick, violent shake.

"Maybe you should let him know."

"Have you told Genny?" she challenged, recovering and reverting to her usual dry wit.

Genny was a part of his life he didn't discuss. She had no part of his plans, either now or in the future. What had happened last night wouldn't be repeated.

"No," he answered, more harshly than he'd meant. He picked up the folder and studied the photos again, thus changing the subject. "A family," he said, ignoring the tightening inside his chest. He glanced at his assistant. "You. Bill. M.J." He nodded toward the tall, leggy waitress.

"An odd family," Val commented.

"You represent trust. Our workers are dedicated workers. That sort of thing. We'll have pictures of you guys hard at work. The family—two kids, a boy and a girl..." He paused to let the knot ease out of his heart.

"The family will be pictured in a suite, on the slopes, in the cafeteria, here in the restaurant."

Val's face lit up. "That's a wonderful concept. It says lots more than pictures of models sitting around looking gorgeous."

"Right."

"We can show the kids on a nature hike while their parents enjoy some time alone."

"Good thinking." Rafe took out a pen and started writing down ideas. He glanced outside for one more quick check on Genny before he got back to work.

He saw her striding off toward the town houses. Dev-eraux had gone back to shoveling snow. He wasn't going with her.

Rafe frowned. A heavy pounding started in his chest. She was going to walk up the path and through those woods alone. There was little possibility of danger, he reminded himself.

People were coming off the slopes and heading for their rooms. It was almost four. The lifts would be closing in a few minutes. The sun had already sunk behind the mountain peak, casting long, purple shadows across the snow.

An urgent restlessness came over him. He put the pen away and handed the folder to Val. "I have to go," he said. "We'll talk more on this tomorrow."

He barely answered her farewell before he was on his feet and heading for the office to grab the down vest he usually wore during his frequent tours of the operations. When he turned at the Y, he started jogging.

His need to see Genny, to make sure she was all right, overcame all other thoughts. He scanned the woods constantly as he passed tired skiers on the upward path.

"Wish they had a chair lift up here," someone remarked, drawing laughter from his companions as he slogged along with his skis over his shoulder.

Rafe passed them without a second glance. His heart was beating hard now. Worry gnawed at him—a gut feeling that all was not well. He couldn't explain it, but he recognized it. He knew Genny was in danger!

Genny eased down into the bubbling water. At first, it was hot, then her body adjusted. The heat penetrated, soothing the tight muscles and lessening her headache.

Too bad there wasn't something equally effective for heartache, she mused. She sighed, feeling the familiar heaviness within, as if her spirit had lost its buoyancy.

She pulled a fluffy towel over for a pillow and rested her head on it. She gazed out the wide windows set at right angles to each other and meeting at the corner.

High above the ground and facing the woods, the spa was situated for maximum privacy from others, but with a magnificent view of the mountain peaks above the wooded slopes. No wonder Rafe had chosen this place. It was like being in a world of one's own.

Or part of a Christmas scene, she reflected, her gaze sweeping over the snow-covered pines and firs.

Christmas. A special time.

Letting her mind drift into a soft nothingness, she watched the shadows deepen into shades of twilight. Night came so soon to the mountains.

"So here you are," an annoyed male voice said.

Genny sat up with a jerk, her body at once tight with tension again. Rafe stood in the doorway, his hands on his hips, his expression clearly vexed with her.

"Why didn't you answer when I called?" he demanded.

"I didn't hear—"

"Or did you want me to find you like this?" He waved a hand at her obvious lack of attire.

She felt his anger as an additional weight, bringing her back to grim reality. If he felt this way after the wonder they'd shared last night, maybe she should give up...just pack up her tent and slip silently away.

His face changed as he looked her over. She felt the heat of his stare like a caress, as he looked at her damp hair spread out over the towel and slowly let his gaze roam downward, over her mouth, along her throat and to the rise of her breasts above the churning water of the spa.

"Is this an invitation for me to join you?" he asked with a cruel leer.

"Not if it fills you with loathing," she said with a tremor in her voice that she couldn't hide.

He closed his eyes and spun away. When he hit the door frame, a resounding smack with his fist, she flinched involuntarily.

Rafe wanted her...but he hated her for it.

Unable to take any more, she grabbed the towel and sprang from the tub. Hands shaking, she wrapped the terry cloth around her and tucked the end under her arm.

"Let me by," she requested. Her voice was husky, filled with suppressed tears that she wouldn't let fall.

He turned toward her and moved aside. Her heart was a sledgehammer in her chest, beating her love into pieces. Carefully, she maneuvered past him and headed for the atrium door.

Before she could dash for her room, he was there, blocking her way, his arm across the opening. She stopped and darted a glance at his bleak countenance.

"Don't," he said in a low growl. "Don't go."

"I—I have to. You don't want me. You...you hate..."

"No!"

She pressed the back of her hand against her lips.

"I need you. The warmth... I can't give it up." He sounded defeated. "I've thought of you all day."

The silence stretched between them, harsh and unrelenting.

He touched her bare shoulder above the towel. "Don't leave me out here in the cold."

"I don't know what you want from me," she protested.

"God help me, I don't, either."

His arms slipped around her waist. She felt a shudder go through his tall, strong frame. Then he bent and kissed the bare expanse of skin between her throat and her breasts. Her breath caught sharply. When she breathed out, it was with an audible gasp as he licked a moist trail of fire into the shallow dip over her breastbone.

Without thinking, she lifted her hand and raked her fingers into the golden strands of his hair.

My golden eagle.

She had invaded his aerie and forced her way into his life, drawing on his protective instincts to take her in. Now she didn't know what to do. If he pushed her out, she would tumble to earth and die.

"Dangerous," he murmured, his lips roaming over her, hot and demanding in his passion. "But so warm..."

She knew what he meant. Loneliness was as deadly as the cold, trapping the heart in ice until it gave up on dreams and merely functioned, aloof and alone.

"Yes, warm," she echoed. "Come into the hot tub."

He held her gently by the upper arms and stared into her eyes for a long minute. She couldn't read his mood. He didn't seem happy or pleased, only resigned.

"All right."

He released her and moved toward the bed. Stopping by a chair, he shed his down vest and the rest of his clothing. Genny watched, entranced as always by the physical beauty of her lover. No man had ever visually pleased her as this one did.

The irregular diamond of dark gold hair on his chest was replicated in a triangle at the jointure of his legs. Hair was also sprinkled liberally over his long, powerful legs. Muscles rippled smoothly with every movement he made.

"Do you work out?" she asked, leaning against the wall.

"About once a week. There's a weight room in the lodge."

"You look wonderfully strong."

He faced her as he tossed the pair of white briefs aside. There could be no doubt of his desire. "Take the towel off."

With trembling fingers, she pulled the end free and let the terry cloth slowly unwind and fall to the floor. A rush of blood to the head made her feel dizzy.

"You're beautiful," he murmured hoarsely. "That day in the desert . . . Later, I thought I must have dreamed it. But I didn't. You're simply . . . beautiful."

"Thank you." She waited.

He took a step toward her, then another. And then he was there, his arms hard and tight around her. He swung her up and carried her into the spa room. For a minute he stood at the side of the hot tub, gazing down at her as if feasting his eyes.

When he stepped down, she released a shaky sigh and let her head settle on his shoulder. They sat in the swirling water until the timer went off, then they climbed out.

The tension had evaporated with the steam, it seemed. They dried off, then walked into the bedroom. He tossed her the velour robe and pulled on a set of sweats.

"Dinner?"

The sound of his voice was a melody of passion—low and vibrant, a wizard's enchantment.

"I suppose." She didn't care if they feasted on food or each other.

A flicker of a smile glided over his mouth. "I want you like that, too."

She knew her eyes revealed too much, but she couldn't help it. What she felt for him was beyond shame or modesty. She looked away.

"Come," he said.

They went into the kitchen and fixed a simple meal of scrambled eggs and toast. Each time she looked at him, she felt she might drown in the fathomless depths of his gaze. He watched her with the restless need of a hungry predator, but with the patience of an experienced lover. She refused to think of the women who had shared those experiences with him.

"What?" he asked.

She realized the pain must have surfaced in her eyes. "You've had so many..." She couldn't say it.

"Lovers?" He shook his head. "None since that day...none since I met you." His smile was mocking. "Shocks you, doesn't it? It rather shocks me, too."

She smiled, delirious with happiness. "I haven't... There's been no one..."

"For you since that day?"

"Before that. Since Tom and I went steady."

"In Paris...?" His voice trailed off into a question.

"No. No one."

His eyes darkened. "You stopped us that day by the spring."

"It was so sudden. I wasn't sure what was happening. I'd never felt like that before." She gave him a searching look. "Later... why didn't you ever call?"

"It was a part of my life I wanted to forget," he said bluntly. "I don't want to talk about it." He reached out and traced the V of the robe until he could reach inside and caress her breast. "There's only this moment. There's only us."

He stood and drew her up, pulling her into his arms. He touched her lips once, twice, then again and again, as if he couldn't get enough.

Genny returned the kisses, but the heaviness never left her heart. She knew the moment would end all too soon and the loneliness would return.

"Love me," she pleaded on a soft moan. "Love me now."

His hold tightened. "I do," he vowed as he swept her into his arms and left the room. "I will."

Later, after the tempest of their lovemaking calmed, after he slept, his arms holding her close, she pondered his words. *I do. I will.* They were almost like wedding vows. She wished....

Rafe stood with his hand propped on the rough trunk of a fir tree. He watched Genny as she did a head count on the hiking group. Satisfied that all had made it back from the viewpoint, she smiled and put away the notepad she always seemed to be consulting nowadays. She had made a place for herself, he mused.

Five teenagers crowded around her, asking questions about cross-country skiing and wanting her to organize an outing. She agreed to see if it could be arranged.

His heart seemed to swell in his chest until it almost choked his lungs. Her hair swirled around her shoulders, held back from her face by one of those push-on sun visors that fit around the forehead. Her visor was red. Against her black, shiny hair, the combination reminded him of a red-winged blackbird.

Her blue parka was trimmed in diagonal stripes of red in front and back. The red cords she wore conformed to her hips and thighs with an accuracy that sent his pulse racing.

He glanced at his watch. Two o'clock. Tonight, from seven until nine, Genny would host the Friday night cocktail hour. Damn, that meant he'd have to wait until almost ten before he could make love to her again. Unless he could convince her to take an afternoon break. A smile curled his lips.

Something hard poked him in the back.

"Bang, you're dead."

He jerked around. "Deveraux. What the hell?" he exclaimed in annoyance.

"You're getting careless when a man can walk up to you and stick a ski pole in your back without you even noticing."

A flush climbed Rafe's cheeks. "You're right," he agreed.

Hell, he'd been so lost in thoughts of Genny, a shootout could have taken place behind him and he wouldn't have noticed.

"Another thing," Deveraux continued. "You need to be more careful at night."

He gave the agent a hard glance. "Speak your piece."

"You're not visible when you're sitting in the hot tub, but when you walk into the room with Genny in your arms, anyone up in the woods near that rock outcropping can see you just fine. A rifle with a good scope..." He let the thought die.

Rafe cursed silently, angry with himself. Some guard he was, not taking the usual precautions. He knew never to stand at a window in a lighted room. That was standard operating procedure for any agent. He'd grown lax up here, thinking it was safe.

"Keep the curtains drawn in your bedroom, too," Deveraux went on with his admonition.

Behind his sunglasses, Rafe could see the man's eyes shift from one place to another, never resting, but always assessing the situation at hand. A good operative never let his guard down.

"Right. I'll have Genny close hers, too."

The other man shrugged. "She's rarely in there. Besides, her windows face the other buildings. Maybe you guys should move to her room."

"I take it you've been scouting around the woods. Seen anything interesting?"

"Yeah. Someone has been through on snowshoes. Recently."

"How recently?"

"Last night and the night before. He likes to stand on the rocks and look toward your building."

A chill went straight to the bone in Rafe. He clenched his fists. He'd have to double his vigilance.

Passion. He'd known it was a mistake to get passionately involved with Genny. Five days of intimacy with her and he was as careless as a boy in his first crush.

"I'll keep a sharper watch."

"Hmm," the agent said, neither condemning nor condoning Rafe's and Genny's actions.

A good thing, too. What was between them was their affair, no one else's, including his father, her uncle, the CIA and the whole damned federal government.

"See you later." Deveraux pushed off toward the chair lift, apparently enjoying a free day of skiing.

Rafe went to Genny and rescued her from the young people, who seemed reluctant to leave her. Laughing, she said her farewells and fell into step beside him.

"That was fun," she said. "I'm tired, though."

Rafe cast her a swift glance. Had she divined his thoughts? He cleared his throat. "I'm caught up. Let's go to the house and rest for a while."

She gave him a provocative, sideways glance. "Rest?"

"Yeah," he said gruffly. He pulled her hand into the crook of his arm and held her close.

"How about some afternoon delight?"

He whipped his head around to stare at her. Her smile was bold, but her eyes were a little unsure.

"Exactly what I had in mind," he murmured in the most seductive tones he could muster. In truth, he could hardly breathe, he was so aroused. Since Monday, they'd made love every day, sometimes two or three times a day. His hunger for her wouldn't go away. "Hurry," he whispered.

She smiled happily and lengthened her stride to his.

Rafe gently disentangled himself from Genny. She slept deeply, her face slightly flushed from the passion they'd shared.

Lifting a lock of black hair, he kissed it, then smoothed it into the wavy mass. His heart contracted with the fierceness of the feelings she aroused in him. He saw no future for them, and yet scenes of them together crowded his dreams.

Since that first night, he'd taken precautions, but it might be too late. What if there was a child?

He slipped out of bed and gathered the clothes he'd scattered in his eagerness to be with her. He began to dress.

Last night Genny had wept in his arms. She'd lain there quietly after their lovemaking, and he hadn't been aware of her tears for a while. When he'd kissed her cheek, he'd felt them. When he'd insisted on knowing the reason, she'd said she didn't like returning to the loneliness.

He'd been insulted. How could she feel lonely when they'd just made love—he used her term for it now rather than argue with her—and she lay in his arms?

A sigh escaped him. He didn't know how this was all going to end. Or when. He was tired. He wanted the mercenary to make his move. He wanted the danger to be over. Then Genny could leave, and he'd return to *his* life.

For a second the specter of a bleak future appeared to him like Scrooge's ghost. Ah, hell, who needed this!

He found his boots and yanked them on.

Genny sat up in bed all at once and looked wildly around. When she saw him, she frowned. "Where are you going?"

"To the office. I have work to do. Go back to sleep."

"I'll go with you," she decided. She climbed out of bed and went to the bathroom.

He noted she looked tired. She hadn't sleep long enough. With her activities as social director, at which she excelled, plus the relentless passion that robbed them of sleep, she wasn't resting as much as she should. She also went on the inspection tours with him . . . and skiing, too.

He frowned, a thought niggling the back of his mind. It wouldn't come to the surface. He went into the kitchen and heated a cup of leftover coffee, drinking it while he waited for her.

When she appeared, ready to head out again, admiration stirred in his breast. She clipped her tote with a small handgun onto her slender waist. She was loaded for bear, as the locals said.

He had to admit she handled danger better than many men he'd known. She rarely showed fear. She stayed alert, her eyes searching the woods and paths constantly when they were en route from the town house to the lodge. Often, she seemed more concerned for his safety than her own.

He paused on that thought. So why had she come there, knowing she would put others in danger? Why hadn't Deveraux taken her to a safe house far from populated areas if they wanted to use her to trap the killer?

Why?

Because Genny wasn't the one the mercenary was looking for!

Raw fury welled up in him. He wanted to smash things, to find Deveraux and beat him to a pulp for putting Genny in danger, for agreeing to let her come there.

"I'm ready," she said, smiling over her shoulder at him.

He put the cup down carefully and drew a deep breath aimed at control. It didn't work. The fury rose.

"What is it?" she asked, her face as guileless as a babe's.

"You. Deveraux. This whole operation."

She became very still, only her eyes showing the instant her awareness changed.

"Yes?"

"Lies," he barked. "All lies. Everything, lies."

Chapter Ten

Genny stared at Rafe as he stalked toward her. She'd never witnessed such cold, calculated fury in anyone.

He knew of the deception!

Her first instinct was to run. She held her ground, her eyes meeting his without flinching. She'd expected him to be angry if he found out the truth, but this...this was beyond mere anger.

"Rafe," she said, stalling for time.

"It isn't you he wants. It's me. Damn you," he said in a tone all the more dangerous for its quiet control. "Damn you for doing this to me."

"Rafe, I can explain—"

He stalked toward her.

She backed up. "You refused protection. We had to do something." She spoke quickly.

He moved swiftly, silently, toward her.

The door was only a quick leap away. She could run...but where? Where would she be safe from his fury?

He stopped when he was no more than a foot from her. "I don't need you and Deveraux watching over me like dogs with one sheep. I can take care of myself."

"You weren't the only one involved."

"Who else?" he demanded.

"I was. I am. That much was true."

"Why? Who hired the assassin?" He reached for her, his grip sure and powerful on her arms.

"A gun dealer. An American... The one who had the bomb planted on the embassy car because the possibility of peace would ruin his business. I was the one who found out he was getting information from an embassy clerk. I told you the truth about that."

"Just not all of it." His grip tightened. "Why the hell wasn't I informed there was a contract out?"

"Deveraux said they'd warned you. You wouldn't listen."

"So my father sent you, knowing you were the one person I'd never turn away." His smile was cynical, but his eyes held an expression as grim as death.

Genny reached up and caressed his cheek. "The ambassador was worried about you." She hesitated. "I wanted to come when he said you wouldn't agree to protection."

He caught her wrist and removed her hand. "I want you out of here. Now."

"No—"

"Out of my bed. Out of my house. Out of my life." He looked at her as if he hated her. "Now!"

"I won't go."

But suddenly she had no choice. He threw open the door and pushed her out. It slammed behind her with a resounding crash. She heard the dead bolt click into place. She was locked out!

She whirled. Rafe stood on the other side of the door. She stared at him through the glass pane.

The pain came from deep inside her, rising until her throat ached with the need to cry. She'd known he'd hate the deception. She'd taken the chance that he would understand. When he'd taken her to his bed, she'd thought everything would work out and they'd be together when this was over. She'd thought wrong.

She watched him turn to ice, his face impassive, his gaze cold, like the north wind. He was shutting her out, as completely as if they'd never shared the wonder of making love two hours ago.

Grief rose, a painful mass in her chest. She'd grieved for her childhood friend and gotten over it, but she'd never get over her grief for Rafe. And she'd never forgive him for rejecting their love.

She fought for control. The future seemed dark and unsure. She felt empty and unfulfilled.

She swallowed hard and tried to keep the tears from falling. Her vision blurred as her eyes filled. Of what use were tears? she demanded. They never helped at all.

The door opened. A strong, masculine hand grabbed her, yanking her back inside. The door slammed.

The tears were dislodged. She could feel the twin tracks of moisture on her cheeks. One ran into the corner of her mouth. The other seeped over her jaw and down her neck.

"Damn you," Rafe said again, but his tone had changed. He brushed the tears away with fingers that trembled slightly.

"Am I to stay?" she asked, her voice shaky.

"Would you leave if I told you to go?"

She shook her head.

"No, I thought not," he admitted. "If you stay...if you get yourself killed, it'll be on your head, not mine. I've taken all the guilt I can handle because of you."

She curbed the wild desire to reach for him. "You're not guilty of anything. We all make choices. Tragedy happens. You have to accept things as they occur and go on—"

"Don't tell me how to live! My life was fine until you showed up." He reached for the door. "I'm going to talk to Deveraux. Stay here. Keep the door locked. You hear?"

"Yes."

He walked out, waited until she clicked the bolt into place, then bounded down the steps with the natural grace of a wild stag. He'd forgotten his down vest. She started to call him back, then stopped. Perhaps she should follow him.

No, there was Deveraux, coming up the path. The two men met. Rafe gestured down the hill. They went off in the direction of the lodge. With a sigh, she settled on the cushions to wait.

Night had fallen before he returned. She leapt off the bench and opened the door for him.

"Dinner," he said, handing her a pizza box.

She placed the box on the table, then got out plates and two cans of soda. He peeled off his heavy wool sweater and tossed it on the newel. Static electricity crackled around him.

"It's ready," she said.

He joined her at the oak table. She put a piece of pizza on her plate, but wasn't sure she could eat. Her throat felt sore and swollen from suppressed emotions. She let her glance travel around the attractive kitchen. She'd felt so at home here. The house had welcomed her. Or so she had thought.

"When do I leave?" she asked, risking a glance at him.

He looked so tired. The lines of his face seemed deeper. A frown pleated a furrow between his eyes. Sympathy stirred in her.

"You'll stay here until Monday. You can move to the lodge at that time, as soon as somebody checks out."

Her surprise must have shown on her face.

His scowl darkened. "You have a job here. Deveraux thinks you should continue it."

"And... us?"

"People will think we've had a lovers' quarrel." His glance was dispassionate.

"So that's to be the end of it?" she challenged. She tried to be outraged, but it wouldn't come. She felt the loneliness seep into her soul.

He looked away. "Unless there's a child."

It was hard to say. "There isn't."

"You know that for sure?" he demanded.

She nodded. "This afternoon, I... there isn't," she repeated.

He was silent for a long minute. Then, "Good."

She opened her mouth and closed it. There was nothing to say. She put down the piece of pizza she hadn't tasted.

"Excuse me," she requested politely.

She rose and went up the stairs to her bedroom. With the door closed, she gave in to the grief. Her tears were hot, painful and mercifully brief. Afterward, she wiped her eyes, blew her nose and lay on the bed staring out at the night.

She'd read too many fairy tales. Real life didn't turn out "happily ever after." She'd thought, when he saw her again, that he would admit his love and declare in the most tender terms that he couldn't live without her.

But he could live without her, and very well, too.

She'd temporarily interrupted the tenor of his days. When she left, he would return to his remote, self-contained ways—a golden eagle in his remote aerie.

When she left . . . She'd go as soon as Deveraux caught the mercenary. She had to be sure Rafe was safe before she returned to Paris and her job.

She heard footsteps outside the door and stiffened. Rafe rapped twice on the wood.

"Come and eat," he said with gruff kindness. "You need food."

Sitting up, she brushed her fingers through her hair to smooth it, then went to the door. Opening it, she found him leaning against the railing around the atrium, his thumbs hooked in his pockets as he contemplated the toes of his boots.

"I'm sorry," he said. He looked up, capturing her with his eyes. He seemed . . . aggrieved . . . sad. . . .

"For what?"

"For taking my anger out on you. I know how persuasive my father can be."

Anger beat through her. "Your father had nothing...well, not very much...to do with my coming here. I wanted to see you." She paused by the steps.

Rafe nodded, as if he believed her.

He followed her downstairs. She resumed her place at the table. It seemed odd to be repeating the same meal an hour later. This time she ate, putting her body's needs first. If she was to get through the next few days, she'd need her strength.

* * *

Rafe paced through the darkened house. The clock in his bedroom had struck midnight long ago. He stood to the side of a window and peered out.

The moon gleamed with cold brilliance on the snow. Billowy clouds were gathering, obscuring half the stars. There would be more snow before morning.

In this picture-perfect setting, it was hard to imagine some madman lurking out there, biding his time, waiting to kill.

If something happened to Genny...

Deveraux had explained the whole situation to him. Because of Genny, the embassy clerk had been apprehended. He'd sung like a canary when questioned.

Rafe hadn't realized Genny had a connection to the case. He'd taken it on, determined to capture the man responsible for the bomb that had killed his friend. He'd succeeded in solving it. All that had been three years ago.

Apparently when the dealer escaped, he'd put out contracts on all three of them, including the embassy clerk. The clerk was in solitary confinement at present, so he was safe.

Deveraux agreed they could send Genny to another house, but he thought she was safer with him and Rafe to look after her. The agent also thought she was happier at the resort where she was in the thick of things. Rafe had reluctantly agreed to keep her.

He finished his rounds of the house and returned to bed, dropping the velour robe on the floor. The sheets felt cold. No warm, feminine body snuggled against him to warm him.

Longing pulsated deep inside him. He wanted her with an ache that wouldn't go away. She was like a fiery star, pulling him in with the force of her gravitational field . . . melting him . . . leaving him vulnerable. . . .

When a man let himself relax, things could go wrong. He'd forgotten his duty once before because of his feelings for her. People had died as a result. *She* could die.

The thought wouldn't go away. It churned like poison in his soul. He'd kill anyone who hurt her. . . .

Yourself? some part of him asked. He'd hurt her with his fury. Her concern had been for him. She'd wanted to protect him.

But she could die. Didn't anyone recognize that fact but him?

He flung the covers back and reached for the robe. He went around the lower level of the house. Then he climbed the stairs.

He moved silently through each guest room, checking the view from each window. At last, he came to the closed door.

As silent as a shadow, he opened her door and slipped inside.

She lay with one hand on the pillow beside her head. The covers were pulled up to her chin. The moonlight slanted in her window, falling across her midway down her body. His eyes, used to the dark, picked out the features of her face—her eyes, closed in sleep. Her nose. The indention to her mouth. Her lips, soft and mobile, generous with her smiles.

A pain hit him behind the breastbone like a fist slamming into him from the inside. This woman would risk her life for his. That fact astounded him. He owed her. He knew that. But the price she wanted . . . the price . . . it was too much . . . he couldn't. . . .

He backed out of the room, retreating from the warmth that called to him, threatened him. If he went to her bed, she'd welcome him into it. He knew it.

But the price... God, the price.

"This sounds like fun, having the strolling players give a benefit show for the art fund. I've bought my ticket," Val told Genny.

Genny looked up from her notepad. "Good. I bought one, too, although Jim assured me I could come for free."

"That seems fair," Val agreed. "You've worked your buns off this week getting it coordinated and publicized."

"I hope it goes well. We sold out of tickets within two hours of putting them on sale Monday."

"Business is good. Usually the week before Christmas week is dull, but this year..." Val shook her head as if amazed.

Genny was pleased for Rafe's sake. Pretending to be absorbed in the list of chores she had scheduled that day, she pondered the situation between them. She could describe it in a word—cold.

She'd missed last Friday night's social in the lounge because of the altercation between them. He'd treated her with an icy courtesy all week—as if she were a relative he detested but had to treat politely, if grudgingly.

Looking at the calendar, she noted it was a week until Christmas Eve. She was expected home before then. Monday, she decided. She'd leave Monday, the twentieth. She wondered if Rafe would spend the holidays with his family... or alone.

With a sigh, she rose from her worktable. "Time for the hike to the lookout. We have over twenty people today."

Val looked up, her gaze sympathetic. "Have fun."

Genny murmured, "Thanks," and headed out. Her heart thumped hard when she saw Rafe waiting with the hiking group. He'd stayed away from her for the entire week.

She couldn't help noting how handsome he was. He wore fawn-colored chamois jeans with a red sweater and his down vest. His skier's sunglasses and buff Stetson looked exactly right on him. He was tanned and healthy and virile.

The familiar ache started inside. Whenever she let herself dwell on him, she also thought of what might have been...and what could still be. Then a deep sadness would overtake her, leaving her in gloom the rest of the day. She tried very hard not to think of the future.

He met her glance with an impersonal one. It was like being stabbed with ice shards. After the holidays, she would return to her apartment in Paris. There was nothing for her here. She'd been foolish to come.

Deveraux ambled over and joined the group. A sliver of fear rushed over her. His presence reminded her of the constant threat of danger. Sometimes she wished they could confront the mercenary and get this over with.

After the hike, she would tell the agent of her plan to return to her life as a translator. It was time.

When everyone was present and accounted for, she forced a smile for the chattering group and headed for the trail. The sky was partially overcast, and snow was forecast later that day. She wanted to get back to the lodge early in the afternoon.

She set a lively pace until she heard some good-natured grumbling from the guests. She gave them a five-minute rest at a point that opened to a panoramic view of the Rogue Valley. Using information she'd gleaned from Bill, she pointed out various rock formations and explained the geology of the area.

At twelve-thirty, they arrived at the granite cliff. Here the vista was spectacular. Mountain peaks, rocky crags at odd angles and the severe folding of the land told of troubled seismic times in the past.

After everyone had oohed and ahhed over the sight, they went to the snow shelter for lunch. Since the day was relatively warm and the sun was out, they ate outside, sitting on stumps, rocks and picnic benches from the cabin.

Deveraux joined her where she perched on a warm rock jutting out of the snow. "Everything is quiet."

She swallowed a bite of sandwich. "Too quiet?"

"Hmm," he said in his noncommittal way.

"Do you think he's left?"

"Well, the home office does. They think that since he knows we're on to him, he skedaddled."

"Do you agree?"

"It's hard to say." He finished the sandwich, dropped the wrapper in the box and unwrapped the second sandwich. He munched on it, his manner thoughtful. "But I have a gut feeling..."

Chill bumps climbed her arms as his voice trailed off. "I'm leaving after the weekend. On Monday."

The agent frowned. "Where you going?"

"My parents' home for Christmas."

He nodded. "Take Rafe with you."

She gasped in shock. "He... he wouldn't go."

"Have you asked?"

"No, but..." She bit her lip to stop its trembling.

"It's dangerous for him to be alone. He'll do something dumb—head off into the woods and walk into an ambush."

Deveraux glanced toward Rafe, who chatted with two of the single women on the hike. Genny tried not to feel jealous, without much success, though. She hated other women around him.

"Ask him to go with you. I'll try to talk my boss into letting me stay on the job until after the New Year."

She took a deep breath and let it out, watching it form a cloud in front of her. The air was getting colder. "I'll try."

"Good girl."

"Am I?" she questioned. "Why? Because, like a faithful dog, I do what you tell me?"

"Because you care," he said softly. "He's a lucky son of a gun."

"Have you told him that?" she asked, a sardonic twist on the words.

"No. Maybe he'll realize it. If I ever found a woman who'd risk her life for me, I'd..." He stopped, frowned, then shook his head and smiled, as if laughing at his own dreams.

Genny laid her hand on his arm briefly. "Is there anyone?"

"No. There never has been." He stood. "We'd better be starting back. Those clouds are heading this way."

She rose and surveyed the sky. He was right. The wind had picked up and was moving the clouds rapidly toward them. The storm was closing in. She felt the cold hand of fear caress her heart.

"Storm coming," she called. "Let's move out."

There were a few groans, but the hikers got to their feet, packed up their debris and started down the trail.

This time Genny let three young men take the lead while she brought up the rear. Rafe ambled along with the two women he'd chatted with earlier. The agent strode behind those three.

The wind blew frigid air on Genny's neck. She removed her knit hat and let her hair fall down, then pulled the hat back on. *Hurry,* the wind seemed to say. *Hurry.*

The dining room was filled, not one empty chair to be had. Genny stood near the door, watching the strolling minstrels greet the guests as they arrived. The restaurant hostess, dressed in a medieval costume loaned by the acting troupe, seated the ticket holders. The art gala had begun.

"Hello," Val called when she arrived. "You look stunning."

Genny wore a red velvet dress, cut *very* low in front. It fit to her waist, then flared out over a hooped underskirt before falling in gentle folds to the floor. A black stomacher laced across her middle right below her bust. It made her waist look impossibly small.

Many tiny, red velvet ribbons decorated her hair. An ornate necklace of faux rubies and diamonds circled her neck with one large stone dangling provocatively between her breasts. The outfit was also on loan from the theatrical company.

"We have a table," Genny told Val. She led the way.

The reserved table had been a surprise to her. Rafe had told the hostess to hold it for him and his guests. She and Val and Bill were the guests. She smiled at Rafe to thank him for his thoughtfulness and wondered if he knew of Val's feelings for the maintenance supervisor.

Rafe stood and helped her into her chair while Bill did the same for Val. Genny allowed herself to enjoy the small attention, although she was a bit nervous about bending forward. She tried to pull the scandalously low dress up, but it wouldn't budge.

She caught a hint of a smile from Rafe as he leaned over and scooted her close to the table. She inhaled deeply, recognizing the scent of his soap and shampoo as well as his after-shave lotion.

Closing her eyes for a second, she let the subtle fragrances play over her senses. When she glanced around, she saw Bill watching her, a quizzical gleam in his eyes.

Heat wended its way into her cheeks. She chided herself for her silly reaction to Rafe. He was just a man. There were lots more of them in the world.

None like him, though.

She ignored the protest from her heart. It was time she was getting over this . . . this infatuation.

The dinner commenced on time. The minstrels strolled among the guests, singing and acting out a story while a troubadour told the tale of lost love and revenge, a sort of Cinderella meets Snow White with a jealous courtesan replacing the wicked queen.

"This is wonderful!" Val exclaimed when the jester, dressed in a red and yellow harlequin suit, stopped by their table.

He juggled three tiny bouquets of roses, then deftly dropped one into the bosom of Genny's gown. He then made a big thing of trying to figure out how to retrieve it, making several grabs, but always drawing back at the last second.

She blushed hotly when she saw Rafe's gaze upon the plunging cleavage exposed by the gown. His eyes met hers, but didn't reveal his thoughts.

Giving up, the court jester bowed to her, then to Val. He gave one of the remaining bouquets to Val and the other to a woman at the next table.

The evening progressed with tumblers and fortune-tellers making their way among the tables during breaks in the story. When the play was over, the applause was tremendous.

After dessert, the tables were cleared and coffee was served. The minstrels brought out instruments—lyres, lutes, tambourines—and played, then invited the audience to learn the dances.

When she and Rafe were called to the front as the first "volunteers," Genny realized why the manager of the troupe had insisted she wear the gown. She couldn't help but notice how effective the red velvet was against the black dinner suit Rafe wore. They made a striking couple—her with her dark hair and fair complexion, him with his light brown hair and tan.

They, along with two couples from the troupe, performed a minuet while the troubadour called out the instructions. When Rafe took her hand and held it high between them, she trembled from the heat that flowed between them.

Their eyes met briefly, then looked away. He was as aware of her as she was of him. She tingled with unexpected pleasure while he bowed to her and she curtsied to him, as instructed.

The dance was enchanting. They stepped toward each other, then back...forward...back... The flowing rhythm reminded her of life and all the tides and currents that filled it—the rush of the ocean to the shore, and then the ebb; the caress of the wind upon the land, and then the quiet; the turbulent pleasure of making love, and then the afterglow.

Lifting her hand, he walked in a circle around her while she stood and turned in one spot; then she walked around him, going under their raised hands. Her breast brushed, oh, so very lightly, against his chest. Fire blazed in her.

Her knees wobbled. Rafe caught her with an arm around her waist. They followed the other two couples in a circle, moving to the beat of the music as if enchanted.

Maybe they were.

She gazed into Rafe's eyes, which seemed more gold than brown or green tonight. In the spotlight that had been turned on the dancers, his hair gleamed like spun gold. He was a treasure of priceless value, although he didn't seem to know it.

My darling. Heart's desire. My beautiful prince.

Her love inflamed her, made her giddy with hope. Tomorrow wasn't important. There was tonight... tonight... *tonight!*

The music danced in her blood, and she smiled, delirious with joy for the moment. Rafe's hand tightened on hers.

They came together... apart... together. It was like making love. Looking into his eyes, she knew he couldn't send her away from him tonight. If he did, he'd break her heart.

The danced ended. She curtsied. He bowed. The audience applauded and whistled their approval.

At midnight, the show was over.

Genny went into the dressing room and removed the beautiful gown. She pulled on her black wool slacks, white turtleneck and red vest. With the wool jacket over her arm, she returned to the table. The dining room was almost empty.

Val patted back a yawn. "That was wonderful, but, as someone once said, tomorrow is another day. That's true. Unfortunately, it's a workday."

"Why don't you take the weekend off?" Rafe suggested. "The place can probably muddle along without you for that long."

"Humph, a lot you know," she retorted with a laugh. "I might do that." She glanced at Bill, then at Genny.

Genny smiled at the other woman, understanding the hope and fear in her eyes.

"I'll drive you home," Bill volunteered to Val. "It's too dangerous be out alone at this hour."

"That's kind of you," Val replied. She looked slightly surprised, but very pleased by his offer.

Bill puffed out his chest, as if he'd just been awarded a hero's medal. Genny suppressed laughter and smiled good-night at them.

She and Rafe left after one quick check that all was well at the lodge. She pulled her wool jacket on as they stepped outside.

"You should have brought your parka," he said, pulling the collar up around her neck.

"You, too."

He shrugged. Catching her hand, he brought it into the crook of his arm and hurried them along the path to the town house.

Snow was falling, a light but steady sifting from the clouds. Genny looked around, suddenly uneasy. They were alone on the path. No lights gleamed from the condo windows. Skiers tended to go to bed early when the skiing was good.

Their footsteps made little scrunching noises in the fresh snow. The path had been blown clear earlier, and there were no tracks but theirs through the powdery whiteness. The lights along the path gleamed on the tiny crystals, causing little sparkles to dance briefly beside them as they passed.

Like fairy lights, she mused. The tension mounted as they followed the path upward. At last they reached the town house.

Rafe opened the door, let her in, stepped inside and locked it behind them. Neither bothered with the light.

She turned slowly. He stood there, watching her without speaking, no emotion in his eyes . . . no welcome.

No! She couldn't bear it if he turned from her tonight. She stepped toward him. Hesitated. Waited.

Chapter Eleven

"We've danced twice—once in the desert and now tonight," Rafe said, his voice like a rough caress in the dark.

"Yes." It was hard to speak.

He held out his hand. Genny took it. He stepped toward her, then back. On the next step, she moved with him. They began to dance, hesitantly at first, then with more confidence. When she turned under their raised hands, he was there to meet her.

His arm glided around her waist. He pulled her closer, but still not touching. Against her breasts, she could feel the heat from his body dispel the cold that lingered.

Tonight. They would have tonight.

She tilted her head, making her hair stream seductively down her back, and smiled up at him through half-closed eyes.

The minuet changed to waltz-time. He spun her across the smooth slate of the kitchen. She laughed, a low, intimate sound in the darkness. Spinning, she caught a tantalizing whiff of her perfume and his cologne, their scents blending into an aura around them. They danced . . . and it was magic.

"I love you," she whispered. "I love you."

"Don't," he murmured, pain etching the word.

"All right."

He spun her around, fast, then gently, and they were through the door and into the atrium hall. He caught her closer and put both arms around her. She looped hers around his neck.

They touched from breast to thigh. The hard length of his arousal pressed against her. She sensed the readiness of her own body, eager to join with him.

Her emotions swirled. Love was like a storm in her, driving her toward him, the need so great it was painful.

He danced them around the glass-enclosed garden. The tiny spotlights cast a mysterious ambience over the scene.

This wasn't real. It was magic. It was wonderful. But it wasn't real. A time out of time.

Monday, when she left, she'd have this dream, this memory, to warm all her tomorrows. "Love me," she whispered.

He guided her into his bedroom. There, he stopped the waltz and simply held her, their bodies swaying. She realized he was humming to her.

"You're singing," she said.

"Shh."

Still humming, he removed her jacket, then his and tossed them onto a chair. He slipped his hands down her back and clasped the hem of her sweater. Stepping back, he lifted the garment up and over her head.

She held her arms up for him. In the mirror across the room, she saw a thousand tiny lights twinkle as the electricity crackled over the sweater and her hair.

"Magic," he murmured to her. "You're the fire that sears my soul but doesn't burn... the hunger that can be sated but never appeased.... Your softest caress touches something deep inside...."

Tremors rushed over her, joining the tempest within. She reached for his shirt and unbuttoned it. The rest of their clothing followed, piece by piece, until there was nothing left to hide between them.

"You are so beautiful," he told her, lifting her hand and turning her in a slow circle so he could admire her from all angles.

"We both are." She returned his quick smile, then became solemn again.

He drew her close. Without shoes, her head was just the right height for snuggling against his shoulder. Her breasts fit his chest perfectly. They had been made for each other.

She felt his hands glide over her back, down to her hips where he gently clasped her and hugged her tight against him. He was hard and strong, sure in his touch, at ease with his masculinity.

He released her hips and turned slightly, angling his body away from hers so he could glide a hand between them.

She held very still, catching her lower lip between her teeth to keep from crying out her pleasure when he touched her with the most intimate of caresses.

"So hot," he said in a hoarse, barely audible voice. "Hot and silky smooth. I can't get enough of touching you... like touching the sun... like dying and being born again..."

"Come to me," she pleaded, needing him as part of herself.

Still caressing her, he guided her across the carpet to the bed. "Pull the covers back."

She did so. Then he let her go long enough for them to slip under the sheet and blanket.

He lay beside her, again making intimate contact. Her breath became shaky. She was so very ready for him. And he was ready for her. When she returned his caress, running her fingers lightly over the hard staff, he sucked in a harsh breath, held it, then exhaled slowly. She smiled, knowing he was fighting for control.

Growing bolder, she sat up and feasted her eyes on his virile, handsome body, touching him here...there... everywhere.

He turned onto his back and pulled her down to him, taking the tip of her breast into his mouth. He drove her wild with desire. His hands performed magic on her. His mouth and teeth and tongue did the same.

"Oh!" she gasped in surprise when he nibbled over her tummy and teased her navel with his tongue, stoking fires deep within.

He lifted her onto him, letting her lie completely on his body. "You can't know...how incredibly...good you feel," he told her, never stopping his relentless trail of kisses, this time along her cheek and ear.

"Come into me," she ordered, wanting him *now*.

"We're forgetting something." He reached into the drawer and removed a packet.

"Give it to me." She took it from him and opened it as she'd seen him do. Moving to his side, she admitted, "I've never done this before. Tell me if I get it wrong."

His grin flashed in the dim light from the atrium. "Don't catch any hairs. That smarts."

"Mmm, I can imagine." She paused and smiled at him, pleased that they could tease during their love play. Before, they'd been so serious. Not that it wasn't now, but there was more.

She slipped the condom over the tip, taking her time with the loving task. "Why is tonight different?"

"Don't ask questions."

"All right." She caressed him intimately.

He groaned and pulled her mouth to his, kissing her deeply, hungrily. His embrace was intense, yet oddly gentle. "I don't think you know what you do to a man," he said.

"Mmm, I think I do." She felt the leap and throb of him in her hand. Knowing she excited him out of his mind brought its own sensual pleasure, she found.

Drawing out the moment, she proceeded until the feat was done. Her breath was as erratic as his by the time she finished.

Before she could slide down on him, he caught her waist and lifted her. He positioned her on the bed and covered her with his strong body. Then he began to kiss her, starting at her mouth and working slowly downward.

When he deepened the kiss to stroke the bud of passion between her thighs, she grasped the headboard with both hands and held on as wave after wave of sensation swept over her.

He laughed huskily at her rapturous moan and ravaged her with a tenderness that devastated her. The excitement built. Rainbows danced behind her closed eyes. She was whirled into a maelstrom of ecstasy, then over the edge. She cried out, shaken by the intensity of the climax.

"Oh, love, love, love..."

From a distance, she heard herself repeating the word, then she slumped in utter weariness, letting her head fall against her arms as she clung to the carved wood of the bed.

Hands at her waist lifted her again. She was vaguely aware of the coolness of the sheet against her back, then Rafe loomed over her, his legs between hers. "Take me in."

She opened her eyes. He had braced himself over her, his arms straight as he held his weight off her. She lifted her hips toward him, and the connection was made.

He shuddered as he slid into her, and she wrapped her arms around him, drawing him down to her. They kissed for a long moment; then he began the ritual dance of completion.

Little skeins of pleasure wrapped themselves around her. She was surprised.

Rafe laughed, a rather nice sensation. "You're a woman most men only dream of finding. And you're mine."

Her heart leapt at the possessive tone. "Yes."

She saw a darkening in his eyes as if he were having second thoughts about claiming her. Closing her eyes, she thrust upward to meet his every demand, and the moment passed. He moved faster, again slipping his hand between them to caress her once more.

The flames rose, and she was engulfed. She heard his voice from a long way off, saying her name. Then the world disappeared.

When she could move, she curled beside him, spent and utterly content. He tucked a T-shirt between her legs. She smiled, then fell silently down a long spiral into sleep.

* * *

"Come with me," Genny said. She stood beside the open trunk of the car.

Rafe stowed her luggage, then slammed the lid down. "I can't." He spoke with simple finality. He couldn't, for whatever reason, and that was that.

"I'll never forget this weekend," she ventured.

Instead of turning cool or cynical, he looked at her with an expression that shook her. "Neither will I."

"You're saying goodbye."

He thrust his hands into his pockets and looked at the mountains. "Don't come back. You won't be welcome."

She wanted to cry and scream. She did neither. "You'll give up what we shared... just like that?"

His face was devoid of emotion. "Just like that," he agreed.

"I let myself believe I'd won," she said. "This weekend... I thought I'd finally found a place in your heart."

"It was my bed. That's where we spent the weekend."

His cool control infuriated her. Twice while they'd made love, she'd seen the mask slip. She knew he loved her—she had to believe that—but he wouldn't admit it.

"You're a hard man, Mr. Scrooge," she said, keeping her tone light with a supreme effort. It was better to leave on a note of wry humor than one of bitter recrimination.

"I never pretended to be different." He looked around to make sure they hadn't forgotten anything. Opening the car door, he held it until she was inside. "Deveraux will drive you to the airport."

He closed the door and walked off. He didn't look back.

She watched him, knowing the stark longing was in her eyes. She couldn't hide it at the moment. Watching him go, she admitted failure. She'd hoped to reach him, but she was connected to a time he wanted to forget, no matter what else was between them.

Someday the memories would dim...or he'd meet someone who would help him forget, someone who wasn't part of a painful past. Then he'd fall in love. And marry. And have children.

Once he'd held her to his heart and called her *love.* She would have that memory. *But nothing else,* her heart echoed sadly.

The agent got in. He didn't speak or bother her with small talk. The trip to the airport was accomplished in silence.

Deveraux helped her check her bags, then waited with her until she boarded. When the plane took off, she gazed at the snow-covered hills, her heart filled with a yearning so wild she thought she would come apart.

She didn't.

When the attendant came by, she accepted a cup of orange juice and presented a calm facade to the world. No one would ever know the price she'd paid to achieve it.

"Isn't that lovely?" the woman next to her said, pointing at the view from the window as the airliner banked sharply.

The lodge was suddenly visible. Tucked into a niche on the mountain, it was lovely and majestic—a beautiful but lonely place for a man who wanted very much to be alone.

Rafe leaned on the rail of the stock corral. Around him, the activities of the ranch ebbed and flowed like a tide that swept past without affecting him in any way. He felt impervious to the world and its happenings, closed off in his own private hell.

He frowned at the thought. No need to get melodramatic about it. Turning toward the house, he cast a weathered eye on the sky.

Snow frosted the peaks to the north of the home place, and clouds lurked on the horizon. There was no snow here in the valley of the Sky Eagle Ranch, but a storm was predicted tomorrow.

Tomorrow was Christmas Day.

The ranch house kitchen was filled with pies and cookies. A fifty-pound turkey was bubbling in its juices in the bunkhouse oven. A ham was ready on the sideboard.

His sister had driven down to Medford to pick up their parents at the airport. At the door of the stable, his brother-in-law talked ranch business with his twin brother. Each brother held a toddler in his arms, the little girls so alike they could have been twins rather than cousins.

His nephew was seated in front of a cowboy on a tall horse. They were cutting yearlings from a herd for ear-tagging. He could hear the boy's laughter over the lowing of the cattle. All in all, the ranch was a happy, productive place.

A lump, fist-size and as hard as granite formed in his throat. A baby. *Genny.*

For a second he envisioned her with a child in her arms, a smile of quiet joy on her face, a look of contentment in her eyes. Hunger burned inside him, making him ache with restlessness.

He had a sense of time passing swiftly, leaving him behind. With an insight into the future, he knew Genny would marry and have children with someone else unless he claimed her....

He blinked at the sudden blurring in his eyes and blamed it on the cold wind blowing off Jackass Mountain north of them.

Heading for the ranch house, he told himself for the hundredth time it was better this way. He had nothing to offer a woman like Genny. She wanted love and devotion and happily ever after. All he could promise was an assassin who might attack them at any time.

If anything happened to her because of him—

He drew a steadying breath. She didn't realize it yet, but she was better off without him. She would find a man who hadn't seen quite so much of life and man's inhumanity to his fellow beings. She deserved a mate who still believed in the goodness of life the way she did.

For a second he clenched his hands as a strange pain rioted through him, leaving him weak and achy. To know someone else would claim all that warmth—Genny's warmth—tore him apart.

He pulled his rebellious emotions in line. So he wanted her. There. He admitted it. So what?

At the kitchen door, he wiped his boots on the mat and went inside. The scent of cinnamon and spices, of cookies fresh from the oven that morning rushed out to greet him.

He poured a glass of milk and selected two giant oatmeal cookies, chock-full of nuts and raisins and chocolate chips, that were a meal in themselves. Sitting at the table, he thought of his parents and what he would say to his father when the ambassador tried to talk him into going back into diplomatic service.

The sound of tires crunching on the river gravel of the drive brought him to his feet. He downed the last bite of cookie and the last swallow of milk, rinsed the glass, put it in the dishwasher, then went out to help with the luggage.

"Rafe," his mother cried.

He noticed she had tears in her eyes and that her gaze went over him almost fearfully, as if afraid the gunman had wounded him and no one had told her. As if anyone dared leave her out.

Everything his father knew, his mother also knew, he reflected. They were a formidable team. He returned her hug with an odd rush of feeling for her.

As he laughed and talked and carried suitcases into the house, he saw his parents in a different light. He thought of them as a man and a woman in love—a couple who'd been married thirty-eight years, who turned to each other in passion and shared every aspect of their lives.

As children, he and Rachel had resented being sent off to boarding schools so their mother could devote herself to their father's career. They'd felt abandoned... by her. Certainly they'd blamed her more than their father.

Now he saw her as a woman who put her husband first—an intelligent woman who was capable in her own right. He laughed silently. His mom could take over any post in the world and handle the job. That realization gave him a certain sense of pride.

Maybe he was growing up, he mocked.

"So how's the skiing business?" his father asked later when the entire clan was settled in the family room, the kids sitting on the floor finishing their cookies and milk.

"This is the best year yet. Snow helps a lot, we've found. Skiers prefer it over bare rock."

That drew a laugh.

"So... you're planning on staying there?" His mother had spoken rather hesitantly.

"Yes." He felt the barriers slam into place.

Rachel stood. "All right, gang. Time to get back to work. Let's see how the tagging is coming along."

She herded her family expertly out the door, leaving her brother alone to face their folks. She gave him a sympathetic smile as she helped the children into coats and mittens. Kerrigan, her husband, pretended not to notice the tension in the air.

The house was quiet after they left, except for a Christmas record playing softly on the stereo. "Joy To The World" seemed out of place all at once.

Rafe glanced at his mother, then his father. He held the older man's gaze without blinking.

"There's a chargé d'affaires position opening in Germany," the ambassador said, not deterred by his son's lack of encouragement.

A beat of silence followed the statement.

"It could be yours," Mr. Barrett finished.

"Thanks, but no thanks." Oddly, Rafe felt no anger as he usually did at the meddling in his life. He simply felt...out of it. He realized he didn't have to argue. He could simply choose his own path and stick with it.

His father frowned. Rafe saw his mother lay a hand on her husband's arm, as if to warn him to watch his temper.

Rafe almost smiled. He and the old man had butted heads more than once in the past—every time they'd met for the past three years, in fact.

As if sensing his son's rueful humor, the ambassador's lips thinned as his ire grew. "So you prefer to waste your talent on that resort instead of where you rightfully belong."

Rafe stood, his hands thrust into his pockets. "I prefer to spend my life in work I like. It might even be doing some good in the world—giving people a place to relax and enjoy themselves with their families."

"You're one of the best situation analysts the corps has ever seen," his father told him.

Rafe chose his words carefully. "I gave thirty-two years of my life to the service. Rachel and I gave up our childhoods for it while you soothed the trouble spots of the world. Isn't it time we were allowed to gracefully retire?"

His parents looked so stunned at this interpretation of their children's lives, it was almost comical.

"You had the very best of schools," his mother said.

"Yes, but we didn't have a home." He spoke gently, finding he didn't want to hurt them. They'd made their choices and had followed their dreams.

He and Rachel had survived. They'd had each other. Now she had the home and family she'd always wanted, and he had a business he'd coaxed into a successful operation due to his own vision and efforts. The Rogue Mountain was home to him.

This revelation struck him forcibly. *Home.*

It would be a lonely place without Genny there. Genny, with her sunny smiles and sensuous lips and generous passion. Having her there for a month, talking to her, making love with her, stirred dreams that he could no longer ignore.

If they caught the mercenary... If it was safe... Thoughts tumbled through his mind. He looked at his parents, saw his mother touch his father's arm again as if to calm him. He could have that warmth, that closeness of spirit, he mused. If he had Genny.

But he'd sent her away. He'd told her not to come back.

An impatience to be gone seized him. He needed to get to the resort. He'd find the mercenary, have it out with him, then he'd go to Genny and bring her home. He viewed this idea from all angles for flaws and could find none. Excitement created havoc with his heart rate.

"What?" he said, realizing his father had spoken again.

"You won't change your mind?"

Rafe shook his head. "No, sir, I won't," he said respectfully but with conviction. He knew exactly what he wanted.

We all make our choices, Genny had said.

He'd made the wrong choice in giving her up. He would always regret Tom's death. He would always grieve over the innocents who died because men were cruel and did stupid things. But he couldn't save the world, he realized. He could try to make it a better place in his own way...just as his father did. But it wasn't the same way for everybody.

The ambassador stood, a resigned smile on his face. "I won't bring this up again." He held out his hand.

Rafe took his father's hand. The ambassador had worked with people all over the world. He knew when to push and when it was time to move on to other things.

"Thank you." Rafe swallowed as unexpected emotion for his father filled him.

He didn't know who moved first, but somehow he was in the older man's arms and they were hugging each other with an understanding they'd never reached in the past, even when they'd worked on the same projects.

"Well," Mrs. Barrett remarked. "It must be time to turn on the Christmas tree lights." She patted moisture from her eyes and gave them a trembly smile.

Her husband put an arm around her shoulders. "Let's change into ranch duds," he suggested, "and do our Christmas thing before the kids get back."

When Rachel, Kerrigan and the kids returned, they found the grandparents and Uncle Rafe busy putting more gifts under the tree.

Rachel took her brother's arm and laid her head on his shoulder when they found a quiet moment alone. "Merry Christmas," she whispered to him.

Rafe leaned down and kissed her cheek. "Merry Christmas, brat," he said. He paused, then added for her ears only, "I'll be leaving tomorrow after breakfast."

"Unfinished business?"

"Yeah." He met her solemn gaze and smiled. "It'll be all right." As soon as he caught Mad Dog, then got Genny back.

"Good. I wish you success . . . and happiness."

"A toast," Kerrigan said when they returned to the family room and passed around mugs of warm cider. "To health and happiness."

Rafe lifted his mug. *To Genny,* he silently added. *My love.*

Genny watched the carolers as they sang Christmas songs. Her parents, two sisters, their husbands and four kids crowded around the tall, narrow windows of the living room with her. She smiled and waved when one of the singers recognized her. They'd gone to high school together.

When the group moved on, she returned to the sofa and the magazines lying on the coffee table. Her sisters herded their children up the stairs and into the various bedrooms assigned to them. It would take at least an hour of storytelling to get them settled down and to sleep.

"I'm going to have another cup of coffee," her mother said. "Would you like a refill?"

"Yes, thanks," she said.

"Me, too," her father echoed.

"I figured you did," her mother said with a laugh, her eyes warm as she glanced at her husband.

Genny had always felt close to her stepfather. She'd been six, the youngest of the three girls, when this tall, thin man had come into their lives and wooed her mother with gentleness and patience. She barely remembered the father who'd left them, then died later in Alaska, searching for gold or something.

"Well, Genny-girl," her dad remarked, "I hope Santa gets in okay. The kids are worried about the lack of snow."

She smiled, recalling her niece's fear that Santa's sleigh wouldn't make it since they hadn't had one snowflake thus far this season. She had explained that Santa was very resourceful.

Her oldest sister had frowned at this. Being modern parents, she and her husband didn't encourage fairy tales.

But it was nice to believe in magic... just a little bit. It made the hard times easier to bear. Genny sighed.

"Was that a happy sigh?"

"Well," she hedged. "It was mostly a tired one." She had helped her mother get the house cleaned and ready for the holidays and the influx of guests.

Her dad's gaze was kind. He'd always made her feel loved and wanted. Her eyes misted over, and she blinked and looked away. Sometimes he saw too much.

"I was hoping Santa would be especially good to you this year," he rambled on as if continuing a subject of long standing. "You were always the quiet one, the one who never asked for much. I wanted to give you the world."

"You gave me something better," she said softly, choking back the emotion. "You gave me love."

"It's time someone else gave you that," he remarked gently.

She stared at the lights blinking on the Christmas tree and could say nothing.

"Maybe Santa will bring you a Prince Charming this year." There was a question at the end of the statement.

"That would be nice," she murmured, managing a laugh.

"Have you never gotten over Tom?"

Genny looked up quickly. "Oh, yes—" She stopped, not sure how much she wanted to reveal.

"There's someone else," he concluded.

"Sort of."

It hurt to think of Rafe. He'd sent her away without a backward glance. She still wasn't sure why.

It came to her that if she'd been hurt while with him, he would have had that extra burden to bear—her death as well as Tom's.

Her dad didn't question her more, but in the silence, she found herself telling him about Rafe, about meeting him and the circumstances surrounding their parting three years ago, about going to him after Thanksgiving and of being sent away.

"I think he loves me, but..." She shrugged.

"Maybe that's the problem," her dad suggested. "Maybe he loves you too much. Maybe he thinks you're safer away from him. Have you thought of what it would do to him if you were to die?"

"Yes." She stared out the window with haunted eyes. "The same thing it would do to me if he died. We each make our choices. I want to be with him and share whatever we have for as long as we have it. His choice was to send me away and have nothing."

Her dad frowned thoughtfully. "I see your point," he said after a while. "Your mother was afraid to take a chance on marriage again. I had to work hard to bring her around. Maybe you're giving up too easily."

Genny was astounded by this mild reprimand. "What do you think I should do?" she finally asked.

"Take him a Christmas present. I brought your mom a cat."

She smiled. "I remember. 'Something to warm your feet on cold nights' was on the note you sent."

"Well, I didn't think she was going to take me." His eyes twinkled. "She thinks I'm a fine footwarmer now."

Genny took a deep breath. "A dog would be nice in the mountains," she decided. "Lots of room."

A dog had keen hearing. It would bark if someone broke into the house. It could be trained to attack.

"Well, I happen to know a guy who has a German shepherd pup that's housebroken, leash trained and ready for adoption."

"I...do you think...but Rafe might...I don't know." She nibbled on her bottom lip and stared at him anxiously.

"Sometimes a person has to go after a dream, no matter what," he said wisely.

She rose, leaned over the corner of the table and kissed his lined cheek. "Maybe I will," she told him. "One more try."

"Atta girl."

When she went to bed, after Santa had come and stashed the rest of the presents under the tree, she watched the stars twinkle in the night sky. She wondered where Rafe was. And if he was alone. Maybe he'd gone to his sister's house. Or maybe he had found someone else to warm his bed.

No. He wouldn't do that. He was hers. She meant to make him see that, no matter what! With a heart suddenly filled with hope, she firmly shut her eyes and wished the hours would fly.

Chapter Twelve

A cloud lingered on the mountain peaks around the valley. Genny couldn't see the lodge from the airplane when they landed. She leapt to her feet as soon as they taxied into the gate, anxious to collect her stuff and be off.

First, she got her rental car and tossed her suitbag and luggage into it, then she went to claim the puppy.

In the car, she set the pet carrier on the front seat and talked to the German shepherd during the twenty-six mile drive to the resort. She was glad to see the roads were clear of snow. The traffic was heavy as skiers headed for the slopes.

Christmas Day. She wondered if the holiday would bring her heart's desire as it had for her nieces that morning.

She covered a yawn. The adults hadn't gone to bed until after midnight. The kids had gotten them up at five.

Genny was still sleepy...and more than a little apprehensive.

"Well, Sport," she said to the dog. "We're here."

She drove up to the town houses and parked in front of Rafe's garage, which was built into the hillside on the lowest level of the house. She snapped a leash on the young dog before taking it out of the carrier. She and the dog followed the snow-covered walk to the porch leading into the kitchen rather than going to the front door.

Rafe was sitting at the table, reading the paper. He glanced up when she appeared at the top of the steps. Her heart pounded as they looked at each other through the window.

The dog glanced up at her as if wondering why they were standing out in the cold. She crossed the porch and turned the knob. It was locked.

Rafe threw the paper down and came to the door. He unsnapped the dead bolt and let her in. He started to say something, but the words were forgotten when the four-month old shepherd bounded over the threshold and sniffed intently at his boots, then his jeans.

"Is this your guard dog?" he asked with a mocking smile.

She shook her head. "Your Christmas present." She thrust the leash into his hand and proceeded into the room.

Rafe's head whipped up, and he glared at her while he slammed the door, shutting out the draft of frigid air. "What the hell am I supposed to do with a dog?"

"Oh, the usual. Feed it. Walk it. Talk to it." She tried to sound nonchalant in the face of his palpable temper. "A dog is good company on a cold night."

"What about you?"

"What about me?"

His eyes narrowed as they looked her over. She wondered what he thought of her outfit. Her mother had made it—a red, wool, three-piece suit that fit precisely and made her feel glamorous and sexy. The white silk blouse with lace-edged ruffles was a present from her dad.

Her older sister had restyled her hair into a long pageboy, parted on one side, with bangs brushed across her forehead. She wore a red bandeau to hold it back from her face.

"Who's keeping you company on cold nights?" he asked.

She was so astounded by the question, she couldn't think of a reply. Then she smiled. "The job's open. You can have it."

He gave her a lethal frown, but she held her ground, refusing to back down from his anger.

He changed the subject. "What are you doing back here?" His tone made it plain she wasn't welcome.

"I had to bring the present in person. I wanted it to be a surprise. May I have a cup of coffee?"

"Help yourself," he said in a growl.

"I love it when you talk like that," she quipped. "Sort of low and gravelly voiced. Makes me think of cold nights in a warm bed and quiet conversation in the dark." She paused to let that image implant itself in his mind. Going over to the counter, she poured the coffee.

He heaved an exasperated sigh.

She turned and leaned against the counter, holding the mug in both hands while she peered at him over the rim. He dropped the leash and returned to his chair. He lifted his cup, then peered into it with a frown.

"Here, let me." She grabbed the pot and refilled his cup.

Returning to the counter, she took up her position. The dog busily scoped out the place, his nose working overtime as he moved from one item to another. He went into the atrium hall.

"I hope that mutt is reliable," Rafe muttered, giving her a threatening glance.

"If you mean, housebroken, he is. He's also a registered German shepherd and very intelligent. Be careful what you say or you'll hurt his feelings."

Rafe's snort indicated what he thought of the dog's feelings. "What's his name?"

"Well, the trainer called him Sport." At another snort, she added pointedly, "He's your dog. You name him." She went to the table and took a chair opposite her stone-faced host.

He set his cup down with a little bang. "I don't want a dog." He paused. "I thought you were going back to Paris."

"I couldn't stay away," she said simply.

Rafe thrust his chair back and paced the room. "Dammit, Genny, it isn't safe for you here. Deveraux can sneak you out and hide you away until this is over—"

"I wanted to come!" She stood and faced him. "It's my choice. *I* decided to take the risk."

He closed his eyes and pinched the bridge of his nose as if he had a raging headache. When he looked at her, it was with great weariness in his expression. "What if you die? Have you thought of that?" His tone was as frigid as an Arctic blast.

"Yes," she admitted. "I can face that... and the possibility that he might get to you."

A tense silence ensued.

"There's no reasoning with you." He shook his head. "I tried to do the right thing. I sent you away, but you came back. I don't know what else to do."

"Let me stay," she suggested. Her breath caught painfully in her throat. "Make love to me."

"It's only sex," he said harshly. "I admit it's good between us, but the price may be more than you want to pay."

"It's love," she corrected softly. "No price is too high."

"God, you're impossible."

"So I've been told." She waited.

He stood at the window and stared at the valley. "You stay at the lodge. You can have your job back."

"Oh." She was disappointed. He wasn't going to take her back into his home, or his bed, it seemed.

The dog bounded back into the room. He paused by Genny and licked her hand, then went to Rafe, whimpering softly as he sat beside the man.

"He likes you," Genny commented. "He wants you to pet him." She walked to the door. "It's time he went for a walk." She left them there, the man and the dog, in the kitchen.

Rafe dropped to his haunches and looked the dog over. It appeared he had a pet whether he wanted one or not. "Sport?" he said, trying the name.

The young dog wagged its tail with an excited *thump, thump* against the slate floor.

Rafe rubbed its head and scratched its ears. He picked up the leash. "Come on. I guess we have to go for a walk. I hope you like snow."

He pulled on his vest and headed outside, following Genny's footsteps to the rental car. She leaned against the door, looking like one of Santa's elves in her bright red suit. She'd put on her sunglasses against the glare of the sun off the snow.

"I forgot—the lodge is full," he told her. "You can take your things inside until there's a vacancy."

"Thank you."

He grunted at her formality and walked down the cleared road to the lodge. There, he and the pooch inspected the ski lifts. Everything was in good working order, the lines of skiers long but moving fast onto the chairs.

The lift operators thought the dog was a neat present. Val laughed in delight when he met her and Bill coming off a ski run.

"So Genny's back," she commented with a sly glance at him.

"Yeah. I don't know for how long." He glared at Val's grin.

He noted his assistant looked happy and more relaxed than she had in months. Bill had the satisfied air of a man who'd had a good night in bed. For a second, he thought of warning Val about Bill's easy nature with women, then thought better of it.

Hell, she was a big girl. So was Genny. Besides, he'd found when women made up their minds, nothing could change them.

He waved when Val and Bill moved on up the line toward the chair lift, then headed toward the lodge and the path to his home.

Deveraux came over, a shovel in his hand. "She at your place?" he asked, as if he'd been party to Genny's arrival.

Rafe nodded. "Stay close."

"Hmm," Deveraux murmured, a frown on his face.

"What is it? Did you see something?"

"No, but I have a feeling . . ."

The hair prickled along the nape of Rafe's neck. The agent wasn't the type to make an idle comment.

"Christmas," Deveraux said. "A good time to catch a person off guard, wouldn't you think?"

"Maybe," Rafe agreed, thinking of Genny alone at the house. "I've got to get back."

"Right. Stay close to her." Deveraux scanned the mountain peaks surrounding them. "I have one more week here before I'll be assigned to another case."

"I'd planned to take some long walks," Rafe said, a question in his voice.

Deveraux nodded. "The lookout trail might be good."

Rafe knew they'd reached an understanding. "Tomorrow?"

"About nine." The agent grinned as he met Rafe's eyes. "Or will you still be asleep that early?"

Heat swept into Rafe's ears. Damn everyone for butting into his business. The situation between him and Genny wasn't funny. And now he had a damn dog to worry about. "I'll be up."

"Have a nice day," Deveraux said, moving off and getting back to work.

Rafe pulled on the leash. "Come on, mutt. Let's go see about your mistress. Maybe she'll tell us why she's determined to drive me crazy."

He walked off, aware of the amusement in the other man's eyes as he tossed a shovelful of snow away from the lodge entrance. On the path to the town house, Rafe wondered how he was going to be able to resist Genny, especially if she was determined to be irresistible.

The pup glanced up at him, sensing his darkening mood.

"I have to try. For her sake, I have to keep a cool head. No losing myself in her..." He let the thought trail away.

He was aware of emotion churning deep inside him. He thought of her all the way to the house.

Genny resumed her schedule on Monday. She planned to alternate the three-hour round-trips to the snow shelter with nature hikes to the marsh every other day. She recruited a college student to take over the story hour in the afternoon and engaged a comic mime team to entertain at the lodge on Friday night.

All in all, the week was shaping up nicely, she thought, pushing back from her worktable in Val's office. She glanced at the closed door to Rafe's office.

He was pretty much ignoring her. Over the weekend, he had gone out with her each time she took the dog for a walk. This morning he had escorted her to the lodge.

He had listened while she expounded on the activities she was planning during the walk to the office, but he offered no comment. He had maintained a careful distance between them during the time she'd been back. She'd even tried to seduce him, with no success.

That had been unnerving. When she stepped into his arms and raised her face for a kiss, he'd merely grasped her shoulders and looked at her rather grimly. She'd kissed his chin and his throat, but he hadn't responded. Except his heart had speeded up. He hadn't been able to conceal that reaction.

He'd stepped back and held her at arm's length while they challenged each other in a battle of wills. He'd refused to give in to desire and her inviting smile.

She sighed and stood. There was work to be done. After she'd consulted with the chef on lunches for the long hikes and snacks for the kids, she went over the lists with Val.

"This looks really good," Val complimented her. "We've had several favorable comments on the activities."

"From parents, I'll bet. They like the free time to ski by themselves while their kids are in a safe place." Genny pushed her sun visor onto her forehead. "I'm going to take Sport with me on the long hike today."

Val glanced at the pup asleep in the corner. "Why don't you make Rafe take over? After all, the dog is his."

Genny laughed softly and glanced at his closed door. "Sport nearly drove him crazy last night moving from one bed to the other. The pup wanted to sleep with both of us. He'd whine at one door until he was let in, then a few minutes later, he'd want out so he could go to the other."

"Ah," Val said, a definite twinkle in her eye. "I think I see a clever but diabolical plan in action."

"Well, not exactly, but why not take advantage of the situation?" Genny assumed an innocent mien, then spoiled it by laughing again. "See you in about three hours."

Outside, she counted the number who showed up for the hike. An even dozen. She called out the names on the list and checked them off, collecting the money and handing out the lunches as she did. "Here," she said to a ten-year-old who was accompanying his parents. "Would you hold on to this menace for a few minutes?"

The boy eagerly took Sport's leash and tossed snowballs to the rambunctious puppy.

Bill ambled over when they were ready to go. "Rafe asked me to tag along today."

"I suppose I'll have to share my lunch with you," she said in an aggrieved voice.

He patted his pocket. "I brought my own."

"A candy bar?" She rolled her eyes when he nodded. "I brought two sandwiches, since Rafe never brings his own, either."

"Good. Are we ready to go?"

"Yes." She eyed the group, which had six youngsters and six adults—eight, counting her and Bill. She might have to impose age limits since this was a long hike and not a baby-sitting service. "Listen up," she called. "Stay on the trail. The snow is very deep in the woods. Stick together. Let's go."

She took Sport's leash and led the way at a steady pace, keeping an eye on the two smallest members of the group, two little girls, one six and one seven. The parents were also on the hike.

When they reached the halfway point, Genny relaxed. The girls were obviously used to hiking. Sport was doing well, too.

He wore booties. It had taken a bit of convincing to let him know he wasn't to tug them off as soon as she tied them on. He also wore a doggie pack with his lunch in it. The waterproof canvas would also help keep him warm, since he wasn't used to the cold weather in the mountains.

At the first lookout point, she stopped to let the hikers rest for several minutes. She chatted with the girls and their folks, then Bill did his geology bit, which he made interesting to the younger members with a great deal of verve in describing the birth of the mountains as the tectonic plates collided.

For a minute she wished Rafe had come, too. She viewed a future without him as a long drift of lonely days and even lonelier nights. At times over the past two days, she'd wanted to force him to admit he couldn't live without her.

Except, he could. He'd made that clear during the past three years...thirty-one months, actually. Which was what she'd be on her next birthday—thirty-one.

Not terribly old in the scheme of things, but if she wanted children, which she did, she would have to start thinking seriously of finding a father for them. She tried to picture someone from the many men she'd met at embassy functions. She drew a blank.

Only Rafe came to mind.

She fought off a darkening of her mood. The day was bright and sunny, relatively warm. She wouldn't cast a pall on it by thinking of him. But she wished he'd come on the hike.

"Ready?" she called.

The group lined up, and she started off again, Sport staying close on her heels.

They reached the snow shelter a little after twelve. They left their lunches inside and went to the granite cliff, while Bill started a fire in the wood stove. They would relax and warm up for an hour or so before heading in.

The vista from the lookout was beautiful. Genny pointed out the spire of a church nestled in the small town in the valley and located other landmarks for them. They could spot the ski runs and chair lifts, but were too far away to see the skiers.

Sport won the hearts of the little girls by licking them all over their faces and letting them hug and pet him all they wanted.

"May I lead him?" the older sister asked.

"I want to, too," the other said.

"You may take turns," Genny told them. The pup was tired from the hike and well behaved on the leash for so young a dog. She gave the lead to the bigger girl and promised the other that she could hold the leash when they started back to the lodge.

They returned to the shelter. Taking off her coat, Genny spread it on the floor near the stove and sat on it. She opened her lunch and handed Bill a sandwich, remembering doing the same with Rafe that first trip.

Except for the few days with her folks, she'd been here a month. November twenty-sixth to December twenty-seventh. Not very long, and yet a lifetime in some ways. She felt older, perhaps wiser, definitely sadder.

It came to her that she wasn't going to win her heart's desire, that Rafe might never love her as she loved him. Maybe all he felt was lust...and the deeply ingrained sense of responsibility he seemed to have.

That sense of duty was one of the things she loved about him, but it was one of the things that kept them apart. He felt he had to protect her from the mercenary. He didn't give her credit for the same need.

Ah, but life could be difficult. Love was hell on the heart.

She noticed the girls were feeding the pup most of their lunch. She took the leash and ordered him to her. "You shameless beggar." She pretended to scold and then said, "You eat your own lunch. Those girls will need their energy for the trip back."

The girls giggled and finished off the cookies and juice. Sport ate his food, but with an eye on Genny's sandwich.

"No way," she told him. She shared her cookies with Bill, who gave her half his candy bar.

When the meal was over and the fire in the stove out, they started along the trail once more. She brought up the rear this time, while Bill pointed out the various types of trees.

"It's my turn to take Sport," the younger sister reminded her.

Genny hesitated, then seeing the disappointment in the girl's eyes, handed over the leash. "Hold him firmly. Don't let him wander off the trail after a rabbit."

"I won't." The child clutched the leash tightly.

A wistful feeling came over Genny. A little girl with blond hair and golden eyes would be nice. Or a little boy with a cowlick and a stubborn streak a mile wide. She smiled, wondering if she could take two males with the same obstinate disposition.

The mountains were a wonderful place for kids to grow up. They could camp and hike and fish and ski. They'd learn wood lore. They'd become self-sufficient.

She considered that. She didn't want them to be as self-contained as Rafe, though. People need other people to grow to their fullest potential as human beings. It was important to reach out to loved ones and to share happiness...sadness, too...and all the wild delights of touching.

Her body responded with a surge of heat at the thought of Rafe's touch. He could be so gentle, so patient. He called forth a passion in her that amazed her with its intensity. She'd never known it existed until he'd touched her.

They reached the lookout at the halfway point and stopped to rest for five minutes. Genny stood looking out at the valley in the distance, lost in a daydream.

A sudden commotion broke out.

"It's my turn. You've had him a long time."

"No! I get to do it."

Genny started forward to where the two sisters were arguing over who got to lead Sport to the lodge. Before she got there, the pup broke away from the girls, dodged the father of the girls and headed back along the trail. He disappeared from sight.

"See what you did!" the older sister shouted.

"You jerked the leash out of my hand," the smaller one shouted right back.

"If I'd been holding him, he wouldn't have got away," the ten-year-old boy who had helped at the lodge told Genny when she edged past him and his father.

"It's all right," Genny said quickly. "I'll go back and get him. You go on to the lodge. There's hot chocolate waiting for us in the private dining room. I'll see you there."

She hurried down the trail, leaving Bill to look after the group and get them back to the lodge.

"Here, Sport. Here, boy," she called, wondering what had caught his interest. She glanced at her watch. It was almost three. The shadows were growing long already. A prickle of apprehension tickled her neck. She walked faster.

The angle of the sun made the footprints in the packed snow easier to see. She studied them as she walked, trying to pick out fresh doggie tracks, and watched the sides of the trail carefully in case the dumb mutt had gone off the beaten path.

A slight smile curved her lips when she realized she'd used Rafe's favorite term for the rowdy young dog.

"Here, Sport," she called a few minutes later, feeling really put out with the animal. She was almost back at the shelter.

Another fifteen minutes of fast walking and she was back where she'd started from. The dog was there, too. He was wolfing down a piece of meat.

"What is that?" Genny exclaimed, rushing over to see what the pup had found. "Hamburger!"

"Don't move," a voice said from behind her.

She whirled.

The man stood two feet behind her. He had a handgun trained on her. He was smiling.

"I was beginning to wonder if your dog had a nose. I've followed you since you left here, waving the meat on the breeze."

Genny noted the wind had picked up. It was blowing out of the north, which probably indicated more snow. A tremor raced over her. She'd be stranded with this madman.

"In the cabin," he ordered.

She turned and took a step. The pup finished the meat and bounded over to her, obviously pleased with life.

"Stupid mutt," her captor muttered. "Git! Go on! Git!" He kicked the young animal.

"Don't," Genny said when the pup yelped.

Stooping, the man found a good-size rock and hurled it near the puzzled dog. The rock connected with a thump. Sport, thoroughly frightened, streaked off through the woods.

"He'll get lost," Genny cried. "He's young—"

"Get inside," the man ordered. He waved the gun at her.

She considered several actions, but none seemed likely of success. She hadn't a prayer of outrunning a bullet or the man. Her captor was long-legged and lean. He looked in shape.

There was something vaguely familiar about him. Inside the cabin, she observed him closely. His hair was long, past his collar, and medium brown with blond tips, as if it had been dyed and allowed to grow out. His eyes were gray.

"The Nordic couple," she said.

He smiled at her. "Very good. Most people don't remember a face. Change one feature and they're completely fooled."

"Your eyes were blue."

"Contact lenses."

"Of course," she murmured. "What happened to your companion? Who was she?" She went into the snow shelter when he waved the gun at her again. The weapon had a silencer, she noted.

"An actress. She wanted a chance to go to Hollywood."

Genny hesitated, then asked, "Did she make it?"

The man laughed. "Yes. She played her role perfectly, although it was a little longer than we'd first thought it would be." He gave her a thoughtful grin. "You were a surprise. I looked for you in Paris. Nice of the government to put you and Barrett together. Of course, it complicated the job a bit."

Genny reminded herself of her embassy training. *Don't beg. Don't bargain. Don't act the victim. Ask questions. Information could be valuable.* "How?"

"I needed time to get away. If Barrett had been alone, I could have quietly done the job, then left. It would have been hours, perhaps days, before he was found, and I would have been long gone. But someone was always around."

"Why didn't you kill all of us?"

He shook his head. "Too dangerous. The federal government would order an all-out manhunt. I've found it's better to do one thing well than several things in a mediocre fashion."

The mercenary sounded educated and was obviously intelligent. Why had he chosen the life of a hired killer?

Find out if there's a plan. "So why don't you finish me off?" she challenged far more boldly than she felt.

"Time grows short. I want to get Barrett away from the lodge. You're the key. He'll come for you." The mercenary grinned. "Men will do stupid things for their lovers."

Genny felt a rush of anger that this man had spied on their private life. "He won't come alone."

"For you, he will. Now, sit down and stay put." He waved the gun at her in an ominous manner.

Genny sat on the floor near the stove. She pulled her knees up close to her chest and leaned against the thick log wall. The mercenary added pinecones to the stove, then wood when the flames rose from the embers.

She tried to remember the training she'd received about dealing with terrorists. *Stay alive. If it's one man, sooner or later, he'll make a mistake.*

The mercenary didn't fall into the same group, though. He was only doing a job, not acting on a belief.

Request food and water, stall for time.

"I'm thirsty," she said.

He stood by a window, his wintry eyes on the trail, and didn't acknowledge her complaint.

"How did you get into this line of work?" She judged the distance to a stick of wood by the stove, then to him.

She'd never make it, not even if she threw the wood. His reflexes were fast. He'd simply dodge, then shoot her. Maybe.

He hadn't killed her yet, and he obviously didn't think she was a threat to him. Maybe he thought she'd make a good hostage in case he had to bargain his way off the mountain.

His first mistake. She'd do whatever she had to, to protect Rafe. It was her fault he was at risk. She shouldn't have come back for the pup.

The shadows were very long now. The sun had dipped below the surrounding peaks. Fear curled through her at the thought of being alone with the enemy for the night. She swallowed hard as panic knotted in her throat.

Stay alert.

Help would come, she reminded herself. When the dog returned without her, Rafe and Deveraux would know at once what had happened. They would call out the state police.

After a bit, she laid her head on her knees and pretended to sleep. The cold crept into the cabin as the fire died down.

The mercenary went outside.

She crawled to the window to see what he was doing. Peering over the sill, she saw him pause behind a thick tree and survey the trail. No one was in sight.

Should she make a break for it?

No, he was in a direct line to the clearing in front of the cabin. He could pick her off like a rabbit.

Instead of coming back inside, he walked around the corner of the cabin, surveying the land. She dashed to another window. Yes, there he was, putting the cover over a snowmobile hidden in the trees. He thought they'd be spending the night at the cabin.

His second mistake. Although he could see the front door, he was far enough away that she had a chance.

Genny was on her feet and out the door in a flash. She ran for the homeward path as hard as she could go.

She almost made it to the trees. Glancing over her shoulder, she saw him drop the tarp and start after her. She ran faster and made it to the trail. The curving pathway would protect her. He couldn't take aim before she'd be around another bend.

Her heart pounded like a runaway train as she ran as fast as she could. A burning pain took hold of her legs. Her energy flagged. She willed herself to ignore it and keep going.

She had no opportunity to look back, but she could sense him closing in, his long legs eating up the trail, which now seemed like an endless obstacle course. She ran on.

The path began to climb sharply, rising to the midpoint lookout where she'd rested briefly an eternity ago.

Time slowed. She felt as if she was running through water. Her muscles ached with each jarring step. She realized she was facing into the wind. It had shifted to the northeast.

The sound of her breathing filled her ears. Then she caught another sound...behind her. She glanced around. Her captor was bearing down on her.

He reached out.

She dodged to the side and eluded him, but then she was off the trail, with deep snow to either side. He blocked her way back. A smile appeared on his face. It was merely a game to him.

She headed up the ridge, going toward the midway vista point. She searched frantically for a place to hide. There was none.

Coming to the end of the lookout path, she leaned against the barrier railing and looked down the cliff at the stream rushing toward the river. Briefly, regretfully, she thought of Rafe and the life they might have had, then she swung one leg over the rail.

Chapter Thirteen

Rafe glanced at his watch. He finished a letter and printed it out. He looked out the window. He read the letter, signed it and stuck it in an envelope. He checked his watch, then the trail. At last he saw the hikers coming back. Bill was with the group.

Pushing back from his desk, Rafe stood at the window, his eyes narrowed against the long slanting rays of afternoon sun. When the hiking group straggled into the clearing, he looked for the blue parka with the red V stripes running up the front.

Like a kid with his first big case of puppy love, he mocked himself. He hadn't gone to her last night or the night before, but the battle had been a hard one. Knowing she would welcome him hadn't made it any easier.

For just a second he let himself remember the last time they'd made love—her tremulous sighs, her cries of rapture, her intimate touches as she explored his body...and then the heat when he came into her, like falling into the sun . . . her gentle fire . . . her healing fire. . . .

He might have succumbed to their passion, except for the sense of danger that grew each day. He didn't consider himself an intuitive person, but where Genny was concerned, he was.

With a curse, he counted the hikers and realized she wasn't with the bunch. Grabbing his vest, he headed out.

He found Bill peering at the trail while the hikers trooped inside to have their hot chocolate and cookies.

"Where is she?" he asked the maintenance supervisor.

Bill gave him a worried glance. "Back on the trail. The dog ran off. She went after it. She should have caught up with us."

A chill gripped Rafe's chest. Genny. Alone.

He looked around. Deveraux came out of the lodge. Rafe waved him over. "Genny's missing."

The men's eyes met. "When? Where?" the agent asked.

Bill explained what had happened. "I didn't know she stayed behind," he told them. "I was in the lead and thought she was with the two kids she'd been talking to."

"Let's go," Rafe said.

"We need a plan," Deveraux reminded him.

"I have a gun in the office." His plan was simple if the guy hurt Genny.

"Good. I'll get my things."

"Bill, close down the chair lifts and get everyone off the mountain," Rafe ordered. He turned to the agent. "The local police?"

"I'll call 'em. Let's go to your office."

Bill spoke up. "I've noticed you two have been keeping an eye on Genny. Is she in some kind of danger?"

"Yes," Deveraux answered, his manner thoughtful. "I think we can handle it. I have an idea."

Rafe led the way to his office. There he pulled his automatic from the holster and pushed it under his belt. Deveraux put in the call to the local police and talked to the detective who'd worked with them earlier. He hung up.

"He says the sheriff will bring in their dogs and a couple of sharpshooters. They'll track us when they get here. You take the path and see if you run into Genny. If you find her and she's okay, fire three times, spaced by five seconds. If there's trouble, fire twice rapidly, then repeat at ten seconds."

"Where will you be?"

"I'll take a snowmobile and head for the shelter by the back trail. I'll come in from the north. If I can get a clear shot, I'll take him down." He met Rafe's gaze without blinking.

Deveraux was a first-class marksman. If the mercenary held Genny hostage, the agent would take him out if he could get a shot off.

Rafe nodded.

Deveraux headed for the door. "I'll see you there."

"Right." Rafe took off for the trail.

He settled into a ground-eating lope on the level stretches, slowed when the climb became steep, then jogged again when he could. Studying the trail, he picked out the dog's prints heading north up the path. When the paw prints veered to one side, he spotted the imprint of a hiking boot in the deeper snow. From its size, it had to be Genny's.

From then on, he watched for that particular set of prints. Yeah, they belonged to Genny. They were always beside or behind the pup's marks.

A cold anger overtook him. Genny. . . in danger. It was his worst nightmare come true. Why hadn't she let the damn dog go?

No, that wasn't her way. She would do what she thought was right. She *cared* about people...dogs, too....

A surprising sting of emotion had him blinking rapidly. He brushed it away impatiently. There was no time for emotion.

As he pushed on, however, one fervent prayer lingered in the back of his mind. *Please let her be all right. I'll do anything. Just let her be all right.*

He neared the midpoint resting place where Bill had said he'd last seen Genny. A prickle of sensation crept up Rafe's neck. He slowed and moved to the side of the trail, keeping near the trees.

As he approached the turn where the trail opened onto the rocky shelf of the lookout, he heard voices from that direction. He froze, then inched forward, the gun in his hand.

Genny wished the man would release her. If she could just find some excuse to get into her tote pack, she could get her gun.

Could she shoot him?

She wasn't sure. And that was the fatal mistake most people made, her embassy instructor had told her. *Law-abiding people hesitate, or aim to wound. Hired killers don't. Always shoot to kill in a confrontation, Genny. Always.*

The mercenary would shoot Rafe when he appeared. He would do it without a qualm. She steeled herself to do whatever she had to do to protect Rafe. *Please, I'll do anything. . . .*

"I need to use the bathroom," she said.

He didn't answer.

Leaning away from the gun pressed against her neck, she dared to look at her captor. His eyes were on the trail.

She wondered if Rafe or Deveraux knew of her absence yet. If either man came along the trail, looking for her, he'd walk into a trap, and it would be her fault. If she could keep talking, distract the killer, maybe they would have a chance.

"I said, I need to use the bathroom."

"Yeah? You happen to see one around here?"

"I could go into the woods."

The gun pushed upward beneath her chin. "I'm not that stupid," he said sarcastically.

She grinned at him. "Well, you can't blame me for trying." She hoped her fatalistic humor would put him off guard.

His eyes narrowed. He gazed intently down the trail. "Make a sound, and it'll be your last one," he warned in a whisper close to her ear.

Genny froze for a second. What did he hear? Rafe?

Then she sneezed. Loudly. Twice.

The gun cracked across her temple, not enough to knock her out, but enough to hurt. She saw a few stars behind her eyelids.

It occurred to her that the killer needed her alive, otherwise Rafe and Deveraux would have no reason not to kill him on the spot if he resisted arrest. She tried to telegraph a message to Rafe. *Darling, be careful. Don't be a hero.*

Rafe stepped out from behind a tree.

"Oh, no," Genny groaned.

"Let her go," Rafe said. He had a gun in his hand. It was aimed at them.

The mercenary raised his gun. Rafe stepped behind the tree, showing only a part of his face. He kept the gun on them.

"You don't have a chance of getting out of here alive," Rafe called. "The police have this mountain blocked off so tight, a squirrel couldn't get through."

"I've got your woman."

Genny realized the mercenary still had the gun pointed at Rafe. She slowly unzipped her tote and reached inside. Her fingers brushed the cool metal of her gun. She closed her hand around it, put her finger on the trigger and released the safety.

Rafe was relatively safe behind the tree. There was no time like the present, she decided. Without letting herself think further, she shoved back as hard as she could, taking her captor unaware. He crashed against the railing, his body poised comically like a stuntman feigning a fall in a movie.

Genny flung herself to the ground and rolled. She brought the gun up. Before she could fire, a shot rang out. Then another.

A look of pure fury swept over the mercenary's face. He caught the railing and brought his gun up.

She fired.

He jerked in surprise. His shot went harmlessly into the air. He clutched his shoulder as his gun hand fell uselessly to his side. The weapon hit the edge, then bounced over the cliff. He gave her a glance of cold hatred, then swung a leg over the rail.

He leapt.

Shocked, Genny scrambled to her feet and dashed to the barrier. Leaning out as far as she could, she caught a glimpse of his body as it hit the ledge below, then seemingly in slow motion, it crumpled over the edge and fell out of sight.

Rafe ran up beside her. "Did you see him?"

"Yes, he hit the ledge, then he fell...." Her voice trailed off in horror at the thought of the fall. It was a fifty or sixty foot drop from the cliff to the mountain stream.

Hands closed on her shoulders. "You little fool," Rafe snarled at her. "You could have been killed."

The adrenaline pumping through her blood congealed to fury. She turned on him. "So could you...when you stepped out from behind that tree...you...he could have shot you."

Rafe returned her glare. "I had to draw his fire from you. If you hadn't chased that damn dog, you wouldn't have gotten yourself into this mess."

The fury went out of her. "I know," she said softly. "I just didn't think. I'm sorry."

He continued holding her in a hard grip. She noticed his gun was shoved under his belt and that he wore only his vest and sweater over a shirt. The sun was gone, and the sky was darkening, the wind growing colder by the minute.

"We need to get back," she reminded him dully. "What about him?" She nodded toward the cliff.

"The sheriff can find him tomorrow. Come on." He released his hold on her and started for the trail.

Deveraux came out of the woods on snowshoes, a high-powered rifle slung over his shoulder. "Good work," he said when he came up to them. He peered over the edge. "I hope to hell he doesn't get away."

"He was hurt," Genny reminded him. "It's a long drop."

"The guy has nine lives." He examined the railing and found a bullet hole. Rafe looked at it, too. The agent smiled at Genny. "Guess what I found in the woods, trapped in a tree well?"

"Sport?"

"Right."

"Is that what took you so long?" Rafe inquired in a distinctly unfriendly voice. "You rescued the damn dog?"

"Mmm-hmm," Deveraux said, grinning in the face of Rafe's anger. "I'll bring him in with me. He hurt his paw." At Genny's anxious frown, he added, "It's not serious." He headed for the woods.

"Let's get back." Rafe waited for her to go first.

She noticed the bleak expression had returned to his eyes. A chill settled between her shoulder blades.

He'd never forgive her for coming here, for complicating his life and reminding him of the past he needed to forget. Her death would have been added to the load he already carried if things had gone differently.

She looked at him for a second longer, saying goodbye, then she resolutely started walking.

Everything seemed strange...surreal...on the way back to the lodge. She had experienced so much in the past hour that she had no emotion left. She existed in a void of absolute zero.

Rafe walked behind her with an expression like death warmed over, as her mom would have said. No, not warmed, but cold, as cold as she felt inside.

The purple shadows of twilight enclosed them. She trudged along the trail and wished she'd never come here.

Rogue Mountain. Rogues were loners.

She'd never touched Rafe's heart. He'd wanted her, but he'd been honest about it. He'd never misled her about his feelings. She'd done that on her own, thinking an attraction that strong must surely mean they were in love.

Even if it did, too many things stood between them for love to flourish. Rafe was a strong man, who cared deeply about others, who took his responsibilities seriously and personally. He thought he'd failed in his duty to protect the people under his command.

He felt he'd let himself be distracted from those duties by his feelings for her... feelings that were perfectly natural to a man falling in love.

She knew he'd never let that happen again. He'd closed his heart off completely.

She understood. But it didn't take away the pain of his rejection. It didn't make her love for him go away.

Genny stood silently beside Rafe while he and Deveraux and the sheriff talked. When asked, she told her part of the action. At her feet, Sport lay quietly, a bandage around his paw.

Night had descended, and she noticed there were no stars. While she watched, snow began to float down from the sky. She looked at Rafe, who stood with his hands pushed under his arms for warmth. He still had no coat.

"We need to get inside," she said.

The three men looked at her.

"She's right," the sheriff agreed. "We'll maintain an all-points bulletin and roadblocks tonight. We can start the search again in the morning."

The search team had covered the area along the creek, but had found nothing. The dogs had been confused over the trail, and of course, the rushing creek didn't help.

"He's gone," Deveraux spoke up suddenly. "He had a plan in case of failure. Now he's following it."

The sheriff, a big man who was larger than Rafe or the agent, shrugged his massive shoulders. "If the gunshot didn't kill him, the cold should have. We'll find him."

"Come on," Rafe said to Genny. He picked up the dog.

Again he put her in the lead, while he followed behind. Once, when she looked around, she saw he had his gun in one hand, the pup tucked under his free arm like a sack of flour. His eyes scanned the path and woods, forward and back.

She didn't know if the mercenary was dead, but she was sure there was no danger at the moment. The man had definitely been injured. By Deveraux, they had determined.

He and Rafe had found her bullet in the railing, right next to where the killer had grabbed hold for balance.

So she hadn't been able to shoot to kill, after all. That made her angry with herself. It was a tough world. She'd have to learn to be tough, too.

At the town house, she stood aside while Rafe opened the door. He turned on the kitchen light, put the dog down, then locked the door after she was inside. He studied her intently.

"You're tired," he concluded.

She nodded. "I think I'll go to my room."

It wasn't *her* room, she reminded herself. She would be a guest there one more night. Tomorrow she would leave.

"I'll start the hot tub."

The words were meaningless to her.

"You need to relax," Rafe said. "You're in shock."

She realized for the first time that she was trembling. Her lack of control annoyed her. So she'd been held hostage and hit on the head and frightened to death. So she had fired a gun at a person. So what? It was all in a day's work for a covert agent.

She wondered how Deveraux stood it. "I'd rather go to bed," she said to Rafe.

He shook his head. He removed his vest and her parka and tossed them on the newel. He found a pill and brought it to her along with a glass of water.

"What is it?" she asked.

"Something to help you sleep." Then he took her arm and led her, as if she were some old granny, to the bedroom.

The dog followed them into the hall, around the atrium and through the bedroom door.

Rafe began to remove her clothing, gently tugging each piece from her while she tried to protest. Her head felt strange...sort of light and whirling. Her tongue wouldn't work right.

Sport, after giving them a curious look, hopped into a chair, curled up and went to sleep.

Her tremors increased as her clothing came off. When she was naked, Rafe guided her into the spa room, flicked the switch and saw that she was submerged in the hot, churning water right up to her neck. He put a towel behind her head.

She lay back and closed her eyes. The last of the adrenaline faded from her bloodstream. Fatigue closed in.

Suddenly she was lifted and resettled. She tried to open her eyes. It was an effort. Rafe returned her solemn stare.

"I...this isn't a good idea," she finally managed to get out.

"I think it is." He guided her head to his shoulder. "Rest, Genny. Facing death isn't easy."

A sob shook her. "You could have been killed."

"Shh, it's over. We're safe, thanks in no small part to you."

"It was my fault," she confessed, guilt eating at her. "If I hadn't gone after the dog, he wouldn't have caught me. I...you could have been killed." The fear mounted in her, worse now than when the drama had taken place.

"You're in reaction," Rafe told her. "Try to let it go. Cry if you can. It sometimes helps."

"Does it?" she asked. "Have you ever let go? You didn't when we got the news about Tom. Or later, at the funeral."

"No, I didn't cry then." He sounded grim, tired, sad.

He stroked her hair and held her close. She realized he wore bathing trunks. Reaching up, she ran her fingers into his hair. Desperation took hold of her. All her fears coalesced into one ache inside.

"I need you," she whispered.

"You're tired. The pill I gave you...you'll be asleep in a minute." His voice was a husky rumble from deep in his chest.

She felt the vibration against her breasts and pressed closer. "It hurts, to need someone."

"Genny, don't. You don't know what you're saying." He made a sound like a groan.

Anguish swept through her. "You'll never want me," she said, giving up. She buried her face against his neck.

"I want you too much."

"You don't. You say that, but then you send me away—" She stopped the runaway words, remembering that she was going to be tough from now on.

Don't beg. Don't act the victim.

When she quieted, he wrapped his arms around her, holding her close. The world dimmed. Vaguely she was aware of the snow falling outside the windows. He'd left the lights off in the room, and the lamps out on the lawn formed hazy spheres of light filled with big, white flakes.

The trembling went away, and she rested. Finally she could keep her eyes open no longer.

She woke briefly when he lifted her out of the water. He helped her dry off. Then she was in bed . . . his bed . . . and he joined her. Again his arms enclosed her, holding her safe from the world.

For the moment, she didn't have to be tough.

She woke slowly, reluctant to open her eyes. A warm, wet tongue touched her face. Her eyes snapped open.

Sport lay next to her, his head on her pillow. He wagged his tail when she looked at him. She patted him, then rose.

A blush flamed in her cheeks when she realized she was naked. Rafe's robe was on the chair. She put it on and headed for her room.

Rafe was in the kitchen. He glanced up, gave her a serious perusal—like a doctor with a patient who'd barely made it through some terrible illness and might have a relapse at any moment—then smiled at her.

"Waffles in ten minutes," he said.

She dashed up the steps and headed for the shower. Fifteen minutes later she reappeared, dressed in black slacks and a blue sweater, a matching bandeau holding her hair back.

Rafe put plates and forks on the table. The juice and coffee were in place. He held her chair for her.

Rather self-consciously, she took her place. What had she said last night? That pill had made her so dizzy. She could recall a sense of desperation and despair . . . and longing . . . always the longing.

"This looks delicious," she complimented, calling on the poise she'd learned from her embassy work to get her through this one last hour.

The meal was perfect. He had even warmed the syrup. Someday he'd make a thoughtful husband. For some woman. Maybe.

She put her fork down. "I'm almost packed," she announced. "Would you give the sheriff my parents' number? I'll stay with them until after the first of the year."

He threw down his fork with a clatter of silver on stoneware. He looked grim. "So it ends, just like that."

She didn't know what to say.

He shoved his chair back, rose and paced the room. She watched him warily, unable to read his expression. Men were such strange creatures.

"I'm sorry I barged into your life," she said. "I realize now that it was a..." She couldn't say it. She couldn't call her feelings for him, her need to see him, a mistake.

She'd come there to find out if there was a future for them. Now she knew there wasn't. It was time to leave.

That seemed simple enough, yet it was so complex. Love. It was such a complicated emotion.

"What about the dog?" he demanded.

She glanced at Rafe. He stood looking out the window at the blanket of new snow, pristine white, unmarred by footprints. He wore jeans and a black, red and gold striped flannel shirt. A handsome man, she thought, one who needed no other.

The vague memory of his arms holding her and his strong body curled around hers returned to her. She hadn't dreamed it. He had taken her to his bed last night. She'd felt safe with him. That's why he'd done it.

"If you don't want him, I'll take him with me," she answered. The pup would be company when she was lonely. She smiled wryly. When *wouldn't* she be lonely?

"No," Rafe said.

She was taken aback at the sharpness in the word. "Oh, then you are going to keep him," she concluded, her mood switching to disappointment at losing the dog. She took a firm grip on her wavering poise.

He stalked across the room. "No," he repeated. "You can't have the dog. He's my present. If you want him, you'll have to stay, too."

She blinked up at him, wide-eyed, confused.

He put his hands on her shoulders and lifted her from the chair. A shudder went through him. "I could have lost you," he said hoarsely, looking at her as if he'd devour her on the spot. "Yesterday... I could have lost you."

The bleakness of despair was in his eyes. She didn't know how to dispel it. "You saved me."

By drawing the mercenary's attention to himself, by stepping out from behind that tree and risking his own life for hers.

"I was so frightened," she murmured. "He could have killed you." She gripped his shirt and pressed her forehead against him.

"You were the one who took the risk. When I saw you reaching into your tote, I nearly had a stroke. I knew what you were thinking." His arms tightened convulsively around her. "If he'd seen what you were doing, he'd have shot you without a second thought."

"No. He needed me alive. He knew you and Deveraux wouldn't hesitate to kill him if he killed me—"

"Don't say it," he ordered in a low growl. "I don't want to hear about your death."

She stared at him, at the anguish in his eyes, and realized it was for her... *her.* "Rafe?"

His long fingers began to trace patterns on her throat. He felt her pulse, which started to throb madly. He closed his eyes. "Just let me touch you," he whispered raggedly. "I can't get enough of touching you."

"Like last night," she said, remembering his hands running over her again and again while she sank into sleep. "I felt so safe, so secure. I knew you'd take care of me all night."

"Did you? Even after what happened?"

She reached up and caressed his taut jawline. "Yes. It wasn't your fault. We were both at risk. I wanted to come here. I also made the foolish mistake that nearly got us killed. I'll have to live with that... the thought that you could have gotten hurt—"

He laid a finger over her lips. "It wasn't your fault. No one can take responsibility for another's actions. No one," he added, as if just figuring this out.

"I know," she said, agreeing with him.

He slipped his fingers over her lips when she spoke. He explored the edge of her teeth, the softness inside her lips. He touched her tongue. She sucked at his finger, wringing a gasp from him. Against her abdomen, she felt a shudder go through him.

"That's what you tried to tell me," he murmured. "Before we left the desert."

"Yes." She kissed the palm of his hand and licked it, liking the salty tang of him. The scent of bacon and waffles lingered on his skin. A nurturing man, he had prepared many meals for her.

"Life can be precarious," he warned her.

"I know."

"People die."

She held him close and felt his grief. "I love you." It was a plea from her heart.

"God, I hope so." His arms tightened around her. "I was afraid, after yesterday, you might have changed your mind."

"Make love to me."

"You'll stay?"

"Yes."

"And live here with me?"

"Of course."

"What about your work?" He gazed down at her, and she saw the love in his eyes. "There's a position coming open in an embassy. I could apply for it."

"I've already told my uncle I'm going out on my own. There are important books that need to be translated into English."

"We'll put a desk in my office for you. This is a good place to work." He gestured toward the window and the rugged land glittering in the morning light. "It's good for dogs. And children."

"Let's start as soon as possible." She pressed against him urgently. "I want our child."

"Give me a year to have you to myself. I'm selfish where you're concerned."

She smiled at him. "Agreed."

Rafe hesitated, then touched her breast. His breath caught, then released. He bent to her mouth, his lips barely touching hers, taking kiss after kiss, tasting, sampling, refusing to let her hurry them with her quick response.

Watching her, he caressed her until the hard bud formed against his fingertips. Her passion fed his.

"Come," he said. He guided her to the bedroom and closed the door behind them, shutting out the dog, who had followed. "Some things are private," he told the disappointed canine.

He eased her down onto the mattress and removed her shoes. After kicking his off, he lay down beside her. She touched his face, his mouth, let her fingers glide over his lips. Everything she felt was in her eyes.

"Don't ever stop looking at me like that," he said, a tremor invading his voice. "Don't ever stop wanting me."

"I won't."

He heard the promise.

"I love you," she murmured, and pulled him closer.

Her love engulfed him, and he was warm. It was like stepping into the sun after years of hiding in shadows.

Chapter Fourteen

The sky gleamed softly red at twilight. Rafe stood with Genny in front of him at the deck railing, his arms around her. He bent his head to nuzzle her temple.

"Red sky at night, sailor's delight," she murmured, her gaze on the distant horizon. She looked solemn.

"Mine, too. Soon," he promised, thinking of the night ahead and making love to her.

"Yes."

They stood on the lookout deck of the lodge. They'd been to his sister's ranch to spend New Year's Eve with her family and had returned to the resort that afternoon. Rachel had been very pleased at the news of their engagement and had greatly admired the emerald ring Rafe had given Genny.

His sister and Genny had taken an instant liking to each other. They had slipped away, leaving the two kids with him and his brother-in-law while they went over to visit relatives at the ranch next door. He'd seen them talking earnestly when they'd walked down the snowy lane and onto a path through the trees.

"She'll be good for you," Rachel had confided later that day.

He'd wondered what the two women had said, but hadn't asked. It was enough that his two favorite females liked each other.

Looking down from where he and Genny stood in the frosty twilight, he saw a couple come out of the lodge, their two children in tow. He'd seen them in the restaurant earlier.

The man lifted the youngest child to his shoulders. The woman, very much pregnant, clasped the hand of the other.

He'd noticed the flash of longing in Genny's eyes when she'd watched the family enter the dining room. He'd known she was thinking of having a child. His child.

His heart suddenly felt too big for his chest. They'd be married soon, a quiet ceremony at a small church in her hometown. His family would fly in for the event. They'd return to the resort for their honeymoon.

"The perfect place," Genny had confided when they'd discussed it. He'd wanted to take her to Hawaii or some other exotic island paradise, but she'd wanted only the quiet of the mountains.

It was safe here now. The mercenary would never threaten anyone else ever again. He hadn't survived the fall into the icy waters of the creek. Rafe was glad Genny hadn't taken a dislike to the place after the ordeal she'd been through.

She was brave, this warm, laughing woman. His woman.

He wasn't going to give her the present he'd bought for her on their wedding night, he decided. He'd give the necklace to her tonight. He grinned at his impatience. He wanted to flood her with gifts, with all the good things of life.

During the walk back to the town house, he manfully curbed his impatience to rush her to the bedroom at once. Instead he paced himself to her speed, watching as she paused to observe the last snatches of light in the sky, smiling as she exclaimed when an owl flew out of a tree in front of them, indulging her when she tossed a snowball at him.

At last they reached the steps, climbed them and stopped to look at the river, winding along the base of the mountain like a ribbon of dark silver.

Finally they went to the bedroom. Once ready for bed, Rafe took Genny in his arms and carried her there. She gave him a surprised but pleased look.

He kissed her soundly, thoroughly, silently communicating the depths of his feelings for her. She seemed to understand without asking for words from him.

"I have a gift for you," he said. He removed the jewelry case from the bedside table and handed it to her. Sitting on the side of the bed, he watched the delighted surprise appear on her face.

She looked at him with a questioning glance.

"I had intended to give this to you on our wedding night," he explained, "but I have another gift in mind for then, one you'll like better."

She opened the case. "Better than this?" she asked in wonder.

He took the emerald necklace, the gem surrounded by tiny diamonds like her engagement ring, and fastened it around her throat. He kissed the back of her neck.

"Yes," he said. "Jewels are nice, but..." He urged her under the covers and slipped between them with her, bringing her close to him. "But I'd rather give you something more... permanent."

"What?" she asked. He liked the way she went a little breathless as he stroked slowly along her side.

"A child."

She stared at him. He tried to hold himself open for her, to let her see into his soul. The silence grew.

"We agreed to wait a year," she reminded him.

"We'll have nine months even if you conceive right away." He hesitated. "It will be my gift to you. My pledge. My hope for the future." He swallowed hard.

He wanted a lifetime with her. He wanted children and the commitment to the future that they represented. No matter what might lie ahead, he wanted to share all of life's bounties with her.

She cupped his face in her hands. "Oh, darling," she said, her beautiful mouth trembling as she smiled at him.

He knew she understood. He gathered her closer until they were one flesh, one heart, one soul. "I thought I could never have you," he whispered. "That I didn't deserve you after failing to protect you—"

"You didn't fail," she said fiercely.

He took a breath and said the final words. "I love you." They felt right. "I love you."

"Yes."

Of course. Genny had always known. So had he. From the first moment they'd met...and from this moment on. Their love was as inevitable as the tides. Like the wash of waves upon the shore, their lives would have highs and lows, stormy moments and calm ones. But always, their love would be there. Nothing, he realized, could destroy it.

She caressed him, and he felt the leap of excitement between them. "Wild," she murmured, kissing him. "Wild is the wind." She surged against him and cried out her joy in their union.

He remembered the song and the desert where he'd first heard it... where he'd first seen her. A roar filled his ears like the sound of a hot desert wind.

With a sense of wonder, he poured himself into her and felt the bonds of life reach out to the future. Our future, he thought, and that of the child their love would soon create.

That future was theirs.

He was content.

* * * * *

INDULGE A LITTLE 6947 SWEEPSTAKES
NO PURCHASE NECESSARY

HERE'S HOW THE SWEEPSTAKES WORKS:
The Harlequin Reader Service shipments for January, February and March 1994 will contain, respectively, coupons for entry into three prize drawings: a trip for two to San Francisco, an Alaskan cruise for two and a trip for two to Hawaii. To be eligible for any drawing using an Entry Coupon, simply complete and mail according to directions.

There is no obligation to continue as a Reader Service subscriber to enter and be eligible for any prize drawing. You may also enter any drawing by hand printing your name and address on a 3" x 5" card and the destination of the prize you wish that entry to be considered for (i.e., San Francisco trip, Alaskan cruise or Hawaiian trip). Send your 3" x 5" entries to: Indulge a Little 6947 Sweepstakes, c/o Prize Destination you wish that entry to be considered for, P.O. Box 1315, Buffalo, NY 14269-1315, U.S.A. or Indulge a Little 6947 Sweepstakes, P.O. Box 610, Fort Erie, Ontario L2A 5X3, Canada.

To be eligible for the San Francisco trip, entries must be received by 4/30/94; for the Alaskan cruise, 5/31/94; and the Hawaiian trip, 6/30/94. No responsibility is assumed for lost, late or misdirected mail. Sweepstakes open to residents of the U.S. (except Puerto Rico) and Canada, 18 years of age or older. All applicable laws and regulations apply. Sweepstakes void wherever prohibited.

For a copy of the Official Rules, send a self-addressed, stamped envelope (WA residents need not affix return postage) to: Indulge a Little 6947 Rules, P.O. Box 4631, Blair, NE 68009, U.S.A.

INDR93

INDULGE A LITTLE

SWEEPSTAKES

OFFICIAL ENTRY COUPON

This entry must be received by: MAY 31, 1994
This month's winner will be notified by: JUNE 15, 1994
Trip must be taken between: JULY 31, 1994-JULY 31, 1995

YES, I want to win the Alaskan Cruise vacation for two. I understand that the prize includes round-trip airfare, one-week cruise including private cabin, all meals and pocket money as revealed on the "wallet" scratch-off card.

Name____

Address ________________________ Apt. ________________

City____

State/Prov.__________________ Zip/Postal Code________________

Daytime phone number_______________________________
(Area Code)

Account #______________________________________

Return entries with invoice in envelope provided. Each book in this shipment has two entry coupons—and the more coupons you enter, the better your chances of winning!

 MONTH2

INDULGE A LITTLE

SWEEPSTAKES

OFFICIAL ENTRY COUPON

This entry must be received by: MAY 31, 1994
This month's winner will be notified by: JUNE 15, 1994
Trip must be taken between: JULY 31, 1994-JULY 31, 1995

YES, I want to win the Alaskan Cruise vacation for two. I understand that the prize includes round-trip airfare, one-week cruise including private cabin, all meals and pocket money as revealed on the "wallet" scratch-off card.

Name____

Address ________________________ Apt. ________________

City____

State/Prov.__________________ Zip/Postal Code________________

Daytime phone number_______________________________
(Area Code)

Account #______________________________________

Return entries with invoice in envelope provided. Each book in this shipment has two entry coupons—and the more coupons you enter, the better your chances of winning!

© 1993 HARLEQUIN ENTERPRISES LTD. MONTH2